"Admit it,"

he demanded, pulling her tightly against him, making her aware of his lean, hard strength and his hands holding her fast. "You tricked me into the river because you were afraid to come out for what you wanted. So you lured me in here after you."

His lips found hers, tasting of the slightly salty river water, cool and wet; yet, somehow that kiss burned through her, assaulting her defenses and overpowering her protests. Mindlessly, she wrapped her arms around him, feeling his power and strength. His hands wound in her hair, and his lips sought the hollow of her throat and began to trail lower.

Cathy stiffened. He actually believed she had enticed him into the water to make love to her! "Please," she begged, "let me go! I didn't mean for this. Let me go."

Jared frowned. She couldn't be... not in this day and age! A virgin!

SEA GYPSY

Cathy Bissette was seeking sanctuary to heal her broken heart. What she found instead was temptation. One look at sexy Jared Parsons and her heart was suddenly in danger again.

WHISPER MY NAME

Samantha Blakely just couldn't tell her new boss, Christian Delaney, that *she* was *the* Sam Blakely who had inherited his rightful legacy. Worse than losing her job, she risked losing the man of her dreams.

NIGHTSTAR

All at once, Caren Ainsley was a cover-girl sensation and handsome boss Marc Rayven's desire. Caren knew her fame would have its day— but would Marc's love last a lifetime?

SEA GYPSY

FERN MICHAELS

Silhouette® Books

Published by Silhouette Books New York

America's Publisher of Contemporary Romance

SILHOUETTE BOOKS
300 East 42nd St., New York, N.Y. 10017

SEA GYPSY

Copyright © 1980 by Fern Michaels

ISBN: 0-373-48275-2

Published Silhouette Books 1980, 1993

All the characters in this book have no existence outside the imagination of the author and have no relation whatsoever to anyone bearing the same name or names. They are not even distantly inspired by any individual known or unknown to the author, and all incidents are pure invention.

® and ™: Trademarks used with authorization. Trademarks indicated with ® are registered in the United States Patent and Trademark Office, the Canada Trade Mark Office and in other countries.

Printed in the U.S.A.

Chapter One

Burgundy shadows graciously gave way to the soft pinks and grays of early dawn, Cathy Bissette's favorite time of day. She loved the morning and its peaceful quiet with a comforting knowledge that the new day would bring, if not happiness, then contentment. That was why she had asked for a three-month leave of absence from the publishing house where she was an editor and sub-leased her New York apartment in the Village.

She had come home to the coastal flatlands of North Carolina, and here she could shrug off the acquired veneer of sophistication and return to the uncomplicated life she had left behind. Here in Swan Quarter, surrounded by a loving father and old friends and the lush grassy banks leading down to the waters of the Pamlico Sound, she could restore her spirit and mend her soul.

The soft lap of the sound against her sundarkened feet was soothing, a balm to her erupting emotions. It was a gentle feeling, like when Marc Hellenger touched her and held her close. Yet, she didn't like the feeling now, here in this peacefulness with only the shriek of the gulls to break the quiet and the ghostly specters of the shrimp boats testing their moorings to the long rickety piers.

She withdrew first one foot and then the other, tucking them firmly beneath her, Indian fashion. She would not think, would not feel. But once again the familiar selfdoubts began to creep in despite her resolution. Had she been wrong to run like a frightened puppy? She recalled her squeaky

reply of, "If *you* loved me you would marry
me." It had sounded archaic to her own ears
and God only knew how it had sounded to
Marc. Why couldn't she be sophisticated and
clever like the other girls in the office? They
would have known how to handle Marc and
his insistent demands of, "If you loved me
you would sleep with me." Well she wasn't
like the other girls and she couldn't handle it.
Right or wrong, she was stuck with her decision and would no doubt end up a dried up
old maid.

Cathy shifted her position on the dock to
a more comfortable one and almost knocked
her carry-all into the water. Her heart hammered at the near mishap and she moved the
canvas bag to a more secure position. Teak
Helm's galleys of his newest manuscript and
a romance novel she had promised to line
edit for her boss, along with a breakfast roll
and a thermos of coffee rested inside waiting to be devoured. The coffee and roll for
sustenance and Teak's galleys for mental
nourishment.

She was comfortable here, safe from
Marc. Now why did she keep using the word

safe? Safe was a word children used, or mothers when they referred to their offspring's well being. She wasn't a child, she was twenty-four years old with a responsible job and an apartment of her own, not to mention a second-hand Mustang and her day sailer. Why couldn't she accept an affair for what it was without benefit of that small piece of paper called a marriage certificate? All her friends were embroiled in affairs and happy with the arrangement. Why did she have to be different?

She squared her shoulders imperceptibly and muttered to the emptiness around her, "Because it isn't something I can take lightly." And that was that, she thought, dusting her hands together and scrambling to her feet. A quick run along the shoreline to empty her mind of Marc and she would be born again on the banks of the Pamlico Sound. This was where she belonged, where she wanted to be...wasn't it?

She ran, jerkily at first, until her muscles limbered up and she got the hang of her old style; head up, elbows bent, fists loosely clenched. Her breathing was deep and regular, the tang of salt air perfume to her senses.

A soft whoof at her heels made her swivel, never breaking her running stride. "Hey, Bismarc, good to see you. Beat you to the end of the strip." The Irish setter dug in his paws and sprinted ahead of her, his russet sleekness there one moment and gone the next. He knew if he made it back to the dock ahead of the slim girl with the blonde flying pigtails, he would find a treat in the carry-all resting on the end of the dock. And if he were extra lucky and the girl was obliged, he could fully expect to have his belly scratched for at least ten minutes.

"Look at you, you're not even panting!" Cathy gasped as she collapsed onto the smooth planks. "I'm out of condition," she said, fondling the dog, "but it's a temporary state of affairs. By the end of summer, I'll race you to the point and win it hands down. Here, you deserve this," she said, handing him a salmon-colored biscuit.

Cathy poured herself a cup of coffee from the thermos and sat nibbling on her sweet roll. "Bet you're surprised to see me home, right? Well, you see it was like this: things got a little sticky back there in the Big Apple and I sort of cut out and ran, back to Dad and you. I'm not really different from the others. It's my values that are different. I know this sounds corny and girls my age don't think in terms of saving themselves, but I do. I don't know how to make the bar scene and I don't bed hop. Maybe I'm right and maybe I'm wrong. I just don't know anymore."

Bismarc ceased gnawing on his biscuit. His ears pricked up, not at the words she was uttering but at the tone of her voice. He slinked his way up to the girl on his belly and forced his shaggy head into the crook of her arm, willing her to laugh and hug him like she always did. Cathy laughed. "I have you. Is that what you're trying to tell me? Girl's best friend. Loyal, devoted and loving. You've got it all, Bismarc. You'll never forsake me. However," she said clasping his head in her hands, "you don't make my heart pound and my senses reel. And what good are you on a cold winter's night? Roll over," she ordered, "so I can scratch your belly." Bismarc didn't have to be told a second time. This was what life was all about.

"I brought Teak Helm's galleys for his new book with me. His last book was a million copy best-seller and this one promises to be even better. If I were his editor, Bismarc, I'd take him in hand and...actually," Cathy lowered her voice to a mere whisper, "I just might get to do that when I go back to New York. Teak's editor is moving to the West Coast and my boss told me I'm in line for the job. Imagine me, Cathy Bissette, a little ol' North Carolina girl, being Teak Helm's editor. What a life he must lead, all those wonderful sea adventures, the true life stories he creates. Now there's a man I would like to meet."

Cathy turned at the sound of her name being called in time to notice two things. Her father sauntering down to the dock and a swift motor launch churning through the brackish water to her left. Bismarc, shaken from his moments of ecstasy, scrambled to his feet, barking wildly at the intruding launch.

"It looks like we've got company," Lucas Bissette said in his gravelly voice. "Powerful company, from the sound of that launch. Rich too, from the looks of that motor yacht riding at anchor out there."

"A bit early for visitors," Cathy said, an ominous feeling settling between her shoulders. Her breath quickened at the sight of the sleek launch, bow raised, water cutting back in white pluming arcs as it sped by the hull. The now golden dawn cast everything into a yellow nimbus and she could see the occupants of the launch as the pilot cut back his engines. A tall, broad shouldered masculine figure manned the wheel and a breathtakingly beautiful woman was at his side.

Lucas Bissette and Cathy stood waiting, a welcoming committee of two, for the arrival of the launch. The man's handling of the boat was admirable as he nosed it into the dock and expertly tossed the bow and stern lines which Cathy and Lucas secured to the pilings. No Sunday sailor, this one, Cathy thought, somehow pleased that such a beautiful craft was in the hands of a capable seaman. Too often she had seen luxurious vessels run to ruin at the hands of careless, inexperienced owners who were known to salty, able seamen by that deprecating term as "Sunday Sailors."

An indrawn breath escaped Cathy as the man leaped to the dock with athletic agility. It was impossible not to be aware of his striking good looks which were enhanced by a golden tan. Dark hair brushed casually off to the side and trimmed just a trifle shorter than was the current style offset piercing gray eyes that flicked over her cut-off jeans and washed out T-shirt yet seemed to survey the soft curves of her figure beneath. When he smiled in greeting, it was warm and friendly and displayed a humorous irony and dazzling white teeth.

Cathy felt her gaze narrow as she took in the sight of the woman who had accompanied him and was mournfully aware of her own hastily braided hair and bare legs that ended with bare feet. This woman was beautiful and meticulously groomed. Even at this early hour her make-up was perfect and her platinum hair had the appearance of being styled by a New York hairdresser.

Out of the corner of her eye, Cathy watched her father straighten his shoulders and hitch up his baggy blue jeans; a silent tribute to the woman standing on the dock.

"Jared Parsons," the man said, holding out a bronzed hand. "And this is Erica Marshall . . . my secretary."

I'll just bet she's your secretary, Cathy thought uncharitably as she noticed the proprietary look on Erica's face.

"I'm looking for Lucas Bissette. According to the marine mechanics on Ocracoke Island, he's the best damned mechanic on the coast. I started out from Maine a few weeks ago, and my chief engineer became ill and is now hospitalized in Virginia Beach. I was going to pick up another engineer in Cape Fear but developed engine trouble out at Ocracoke. We made it here by the skin of our teeth and I mean that literally. I'm on my way home to Lighthouse Point, in Florida. Now, can you tell me where I can find this Bissette fella?"

A half-smile formed around the corners of Cathy's mouth. It didn't seem like a question to her but a demand. How would her father react to this demand? She was chagrined to see a wide smile stretch Lucas' mouth as he looked at the woman as he answered.

"You're talking to him," Lucas drawled. "And you heard right. I am the best damned mechanic on the coast."

"I just knew it," Erica smiled winningly. "You have that...that look about you that...that speaks of knowledge."

Cathy grinned when Jared Parsons winced. So much for eloquent secretaries, she thought nastily, disliking the beautiful Erica on sight.

Jared extended his hand toward Lucas and gripped the other's firmly. "Glad to meet you, Mr. Bissette. Sure hope you can help me."

"I'll try. Can you tell me what's wrong?" Lucas asked, expecting to hear a series of complaints in the most untechnical terms such as, she's dragging, can't get any speed out of her, the head's plugged and won't flush, or she's making a sort of thumping noise. Instead, Jared Parsons seemed to have a very knowledgeable opinion of what was wrong with his motor yacht.

"Firstly, I know it's the primary marine generator. We were supposed to pick up another at Cape Fear. The replacement engineer has ordered it, picked it up and it's all ready to go. Secondly, I believe the exhaust manifold is on the fluke. Last, but not least, I think the raw water intake is giving me trouble. Again, I might add. It was taken care of, or at least I thought it was, in Kennebunkport, Maine. Now, I'm not so certain."

"Sounds like you've got a real ox in the ditch, son. I'll have a look at it for you, later today, when I have time. If it can be fixed I'll be glad to oblige. Better be prepared to stick around for a week or so."

"A week! Mr. Bissette, I don't have a week! I have to be back at Lighthouse Point at the end of *this* week. Look, I'll pay you double what you charge, triple if necessary. But I need the work done today, tomorrow at the latest."

Cathy's back stiffened at the man's arrogant tone. Why did men like him always think money could buy everything? She clenched her teeth, if Lucas buckled under she would push him off the dock and that fancy looking Erica right along with him.

Bismarc was in tune with Cathy's emotions and began a deep growl in his throat to show his own disapproval. And then he did something that lightened Cathy's heart. He had slowly maneuvered himself over to Erica and was slowly licking her leg.

"Eeek!" Erica squealed, backing away and at the same time losing her balance, toppling into the brackish water. "Filthy creature!" she shouted as she surfaced with an undignified splash.

Bismarc, unconcerned with what he had done, reared up and placed his paws on Jared's shoulders, demanding attention.

Jared wasn't in the least angry and issued a deep chuckle as he watched his secretary. Lucas seemed concerned and made a move to assist the woman when Jared stopped him. "She knows how to swim and the ladder is right there." He scratched the big dog's head and grinned at Cathy. "Affectionate dog you have here. He seems to have firm likes and dislikes."

Cathy stared into slate gray eyes, again aware of her shabby appearance. She felt out of place and uncomfortable at the man's close scrutiny. She had to say something, make some comment. "I thought you said your secretary could swim. Looks to me like she's going down for the third time."

"She'll come up when she realizes I'm not going in after her," Jared said coolly.

Cathy shrugged as she bent down to pick up her carry-all, the contents had spilled with Erica's wild plunge into the water.

"Allow me," Jared said, bending down. He handed the Teak Helm galleys to her along with the thermos.

Cathy couldn't conceive what came over her, but she snatched the galleys from his hand. "Give me that!"

The gray eyes were mocking when Jared handed them over. "I wasn't going to keep it. I was just putting it in your bag." His smile was tight, almost grim when he watched her place the rolled leaflets in her bag as though she were handling eggs.

"Darn you, Jared. You could have pulled me out," Erica said as she wiped straggles of hair from her eyes. Angrily, she lashed out with her foot, her aim directed at Bismarc.

Jared's face was hard and cold as he grasped her arm, pulling her back from the dog. "The animal was just being friendly. Get in the launch and I'll take you back to the *Gypsy* so you can get cleaned up." He looked at Lucas and said, "I'll be back as soon as I get her to the yacht and we can talk."

Bismarc advanced a step by way of apology to Erica who squealed in fright.

Cathy couldn't help but burst out laughing. "Come on, Bizzy, time to go back to the house." Without another word she turned on her heel and sprinted after Bismarc who had taken the lead. She would have been bewildered if she could have seen the look on Jared Parsons' face as he watched her running retreat, the yellow tote bouncing against her side.

Back in the house, Cathy set about making breakfast. She cracked eggs into the bowl and automatically beat them wildly. She was angry and she didn't know why. She certainly wasn't angry because Jared Parsons touched her precious Teak Helm galleys. She had just met the man and here she was beating the eggs with fury yet her blood churning wildly in her veins. Suddenly, Cathy realized it was Erica. No one in the whole world should be allowed to be that beautiful. Even Lucas, her very own father, fell for her good looks. Men! And, Erica belonged to Jared Parsons. She belonged to him the way Cathy, herself, could have belonged to Marc if she had given in to his demands.

Would Marc have let her go down in the water for the third time she wondered? Then make some scathing comment as Jared had done? Yes, she admitted to herself. Men did things like that when they believed they owned women. She wondered, fleetingly, if Jared Parsons paid the beautiful and ravishing Erica a salary for her secretarial duties. But the sharp hiss of the eggs as they hit the hot butter in the pan brought her thoughts back to the task at hand.

Lucas Bissette walked though the door just as Cathy slid the eggs onto his plate. She said nothing but waited for him to make some mention of their early morning visitors. As she busied herself with spooning food into Bismarc's dish and refilling his water bowl, her thoughts raced. Jared Parsons was good looking, downright handsome. He was virile and athletic and obviously very rich. He was also arrogant and demanding and sported a slightly condescending attitude. There had been a moment when she had actually expected him to pat her on the head like he had done to Bismarc. He also had a live-in woman. How old fashioned that sounded, how jealous and spiteful. Why should she be jealous? She had only met the man, a man who looked at her the way he would a grubby child.

Cathy stood up facing the kitchen window, watching the return of the power launch. She felt a tremor in her legs and her heart began a wild fluttering. Some instinct, some intangible force, was making her aware of this man with the gray eyes and wry smile. She envied Erica and all the women like her. Was she wrong? Were they right, to live for the moment and enjoy it for what it was? Cathy sighed, the sound loud in the quiet of the kitchen.

"Did you make enough eggs for Mr. Parsons?" Lucas asked, biting into a crisp piece of toast.

Cathy swiveled from her position at the window. "No, I didn't make enough eggs because I didn't know he was coming for breakfast. Since I'm the cook around here, it would have been nice if you had informed me," she snapped.

"I've invited people on the spur of the moment before and it's never annoyed you," Lucas said, pushing his plate toward the center of the oak table.

"Next time, please ask me," Cathy said quietly. "Open the door, he's here." She turned, busying herself at the stove. She was ill at ease, uncomfortable in the man's presence. Somehow, deep within her, she knew her life was changing, had begun to change, the minute Jared Parsons stepped from his launch.

Bismarc's loud bark of welcome made her drop the egg she was holding and the laughter in Jared's eyes made her grit her teeth. Even the dog liked him. Dogs were supposed to be astute judges of character. A pity Bismarc wasn't perfect.

Cathy cleaned up the broken egg and turned to face him. "What would you like for breakfast, Mr. Parsons?"

"Anything you'd care to make will be fine. I hope I'm not putting you out or keeping you from something." Was it her imagination? Did his eyes go to the yellow tote or was he looking at the copper and wood butter churn that sat in the corner?

"Cathy's never too busy to cook. It's one of her favorite pastimes," Lucas said affably. "Why, she always wins the prize at the July 4th picnic for her She-Crab stew. Won it four years in a row. Yes sir, all the young bucks around here come on Sundays and Cathy whips something up for them."

Dear heaven, Cathy groaned inwardly. Here she was yearning to be glamorous and seductive like Erica and Lucas was extolling her homey virtues.

"If there's one thing I really can appreciate, it's a good cook," Jared laughed.

Cathy pursed her lips. Among other things, she thought nastily as she liberally sprinkled chives and cheddar cheese into the whipped eggs, and hoped that Jared Parsons attributed her flushed face to the heat from the stove.

Chapter Two

Jared Parsons wolfed down the breakfast Cathy had set before him. She hoped Lucas didn't notice that their visitor's eggs had been laced with chives and cheese while his own had been served plain. She thought she noticed amusement in her father's eyes as he glanced at the cinnamon toast and fancy mug resting near Jared's plate.

Lucas managed to catch his daughter's eye by clearing his throat and winked slyly. Cathy in turn banged the fry pan into the sink and flounced out of the kitchen, then stopped in her tracks and returned. She wanted to hear what Parsons had to say with her own ears. The day any man could bully her father was a day she wanted to see. What would the stylish yachtsman do when his offer of triple money failed to hurry Lucas Bissette? A vision of the muscular man in his natty ducks and yellow pullover being frustrated by Lucas' unhurried southern habits made her giggle. Bismarc heard her, and Lucas and Jared both looked at her. Her father with amusement, and Parsons with speculation.

"If you've finished your breakfast, let's take a look at that engine," Lucas said, getting up from his chair. Jared dabbed at his mouth with the checkered napkin and then pointedly placed it beside Lucas' paper napkin, a wicked smile playing on his lips. Cathy's eyes followed his movements and a dark flush worked its way over her cheekbones. Damn Jared Parsons.

"Any time you're ready, Mr. Bissette. I meant what I said down at the dock. I'll pay you whatever you want, if you do the job tomorrow at the latest. It's imperative I reach Lighthouse Point before the end of the week.''

His voice was cool and businesslike, making Lucas frown. You didn't issue orders to Lucas Bissette, not in his own house or anywhere else, for that matter. And it was an order, regardless of how the man worded it. Cathy knew it and Lucas knew it.

"Well now, Mr. Parsons," Lucas drawled as he sucked on his pipe, "I don't rightly see how I can accommodate you, since I haven't seen the extent of the problem. Besides, if it is that new generator you'll be needing, it will take time to order it. Even if we get it up here from Cape Fear, that's going to take a day or so."

"A day or so!" Parsons protested. "It's only about five hours from here by land!"

"Best you bear in mind that we...hayseeds down here in the boonies operate at two speeds. Slow and stop. Least that's what I've heard said."

Cathy grinned openly. Good for you, Dad, that's telling him money is just something you buy things with, not people. Jared's mouth tightened at Cathy's grin. He had been put down and by an expert, something Cathy knew rarely, if ever, happened to him. Jared nodded, his gray eyes murky as the river on a bad day.

Lucas laid a rough hand on Jared's shoulder, taking the sting out of his insult, and said softly, "Just because we all live here in this little backwater called Swan Quarter doesn't mean we aren't aware of the outside world. We also have priorities, and today I gave my word I would help Jesse Gallagher repair his shrimp nets. Now, Mr. Parsons, even if you were to tell me you had a multi-million dollar business deal going in Lighthouse Point, I'd still tell you that Jesse's shrimp nets are top priority. Just want you to understand that . . . son."

Never one to let things simmer when she could bring them to a boil, Cathy spoke up. "What Dad is trying to tell you, Mr. Parsons, is your money isn't important here and neither are your cool-voiced arrogant demands. You came to us, we didn't come to you."

"This may surprise you, Miss Bissette, but I understood your father perfectly down at the dock and I understand him now. There's no need for you to interpret his words for me." He was angry, probably more angry than any man Cathy had ever seen. It was evident in the grim set of his shoulders and the stiff bunching of the muscles in his jaw. People liked Jared Parsons didn't bend to anyone, they were the ones who toppled others and stood by while someone else picked up the remains.

"If you're ready, Mr. Bissette." Jared turned and looked around, his next words stunning Cathy. "I like this kitchen. It's very homey with all the copper and greenery. I particularly like the open hearth and the overhead beams."

For a hairbreadth of a second, Cathy would have sworn there was a wistful look in the gray eyes and then it was gone.

"Cathy fixed up the kitchen like this from one of those fancy magazines. She's got a good eye for what makes comfort," Lucas said, winking at his daughter.

Jared Parsons turned and faced Cathy. "I guess one could say you're a homebody at heart." He grinned, but the emotion never reached his eyes, they were cool and unread-able. Cathy flushed beneath his steady gaze.

"I guess you could say that. What you see is what I am."

"Cathy, why don't you follow us out in the runabout so you can bring me back and save Mr. Parsons an extra trip? After all, he does have a guest on board and we don't want to take up all of his time."

"I'll be out after I clean up the kitchen. You go ahead," Cathy answered, refusing to turn away from the sink and see those in-scrutable gray eyes piercing through her as though they could read her mind.

Bismarc got up and stretched from his comfortable spot on the wide hearth, look-ing first at Lucas and then at Cathy. Lucas laughed, a great laugh, starting at his toes and erupting from his throat. "Best lock Bizzy in the house when you leave. If we don't take him with us he'll only swim out after us."

Cathy grinned inwardly at what she imag-ined would be the scene on Jared Parsons' varnished deck and Miss Beautiful Marshall squealing her head off.

"Don't lock him in, Mr. Bissette," Jared protested. "If he wants our company, it's okay with me," he added agreeably.

"If we're going to do business, call me Lucas."

"Fine with me, and I'm Jared."

"Let's go, Jared," Lucas said, striding out the kitchen door and leading the way down the footpath to the dock that sat out in front of the house. Jared obediently followed along with Bismarc trailing contentedly beside him. Cathy watched as his big bronzed hand fondled the dog's head from time to time during the short walk.

Filling the sink with hot soapy water, Cathy then poured herself a cup of coffee and sat down. She stared at the cup without drinking. Instead, she picked up the cup Jared had used and ran her thumb around the handle. Her own blue-green eyes darkened at the cup. There seemed to be a faint scent of masculine cologne near her, a reminder that Jared had sat where she was sitting. Her heart thumped as she recalled his handsome good looks. He was definitely what was known as "macho." If only he weren't so arrogant and condescending. She wondered fleetingly who his tailor was. He hadn't bought those sport clothes off any rack, she was certain of it. And, thank heavens, he didn't jangle with clanking jewelry. He was definitely a man to turn a girl's head, and Erica what's-her-name had him all to herself.

But he had liked her kitchen. He liked her father and Bizzy and he had also liked her eggs. She could tell by the way he had wolfed them down. What did he think of her? Cathy grimaced. As if she didn't know. If she were standing beside Erica what's-her-name, even her own father wouldn't notice her. There was no contest, that was for sure.

Darn you, Jared Parsons she thought. My life was just getting back on an even keel and here you limp into our port and already my life is changing in front of my eyes. Somehow, someway, you're going to change us. I can feel it, sense it, and I'm not sure I like it.

Lucas liked Jared Parsons, Bizzy did too. So why did she have this strange sense of forbidding when it came to her opinion of the man? There was something about him,

something that didn't ring true. Not that it
was any of her business, but she would have
liked to know just what his pressing business was in Lighthouse Point. What did he
do for a living? Suddenly, it seemed very
important to know. It wasn't fair, she told
herself, to make judgments without knowing the whole picture. Yet somehow the
word phony came to mind when Jared Parsons' face came into her line of vision. But
now that Lucas had straightened him out,
the two men would undoubtedly become
friends. Everyone liked Lucas Bissette and
Jared Parsons was no exception. Her father
would have the yachtsman eating out of his
hand before the end of the day.

This speculation wasn't getting the chores
done. The dishes had to be cleaned and she
had planned on mopping up the flagstone
floor before she settled herself with Teak
Helm's galleys. That alone was enough to
anger her. She had looked forward to sitting
down and devouring Helm's latest sea adventure undisturbed. Now she had to take a
run out to the yacht and bring Lucas back,
and if she knew her father, he would pore

over Parsons' engine for hours before he made his final diagnosis of the problem.

To Lucas Bissette, an engine was like a woman, a complete mystery that only the best of men could master. Of course, that didn't apply to women like Erica Marshall. There was no mystery there. "I'd give seven years of my life if I could look like her," Cathy groaned as she swished the dishcloth over the breakfast plates.

Men like Jared Parsons didn't look at girls like Cathy Bissette, who had brains; girls like Erica got the looks. Cathy sniffed as she squeezed the cloth, pretending it was beautiful Erica's neck.

What's happening to me? she demanded of the empty room. Why am I feeling so spiteful and catty? She didn't even know Erica Marshall and she didn't know Jared Parsons. She would put both of them out of her mind and get back on an even course. She would pick up her father and then the rest of the day would be hers to pore over the galleys. Things could only change if she allowed it. What was it her old Psych Prof had said? When it comes to dealing with emotions there are no tried and true answers. One is not responsible for one's emotions. They are intangibles, without substance.

Well, the first order of the day was to stop feeling guilty about her feelings and to batten down her emotions and begin enjoying her summer. She had slaved all winter long for this time and by all that was holy, no rich playboy with a live-in girlfriend in tow, was going to spoil it for her.

Cathy brought the runabout's engine to life with a flick of the switch and carefully backed it out of the mooring. She was proud of her ability with boats and her knowledge of the water. She steered deftly, heading out into the sound, loving the salty spray from the waters as it misted about her, causing the golden strands of hair to curl at her temples and giving her the look of a child of twelve. As she brought the bow about to give her a heading which would take her to the disabled motor yacht, she was surprised at the size of the vessel. It was an Italian vessel, fifty feet on the keel, at the very least. Mentally, Cathy recalled all she had heard or read about the elegant yacht. If she wasn't mistaken, Teak Helm had also glorified their delights. Wantonly powered, he had called them in one of his books. Only a rare man could afford them, and only a rare man has the style and the women to match their stunning beauty and excess.

Cathy noticed the yacht's name painted in gold leaf on her stern, *Sea Gypsy III*. From the looks of the flying bridge and the appointments of bass and gleaming chrome, she could imagine that the interior would bring a blush to Hugh Hefner's cheeks. A veritable floating Bunny Hutch, she snickered in disdain. Yet her innate love of beauty and the pleasure she took in the sleek lines of sea craft overrode her scorn.

It was Erica Marshall who greeted her as Cathy cut her engine and secured the craft to the mooring lines of the *Gypsy*. Deftly, she maneuvered her way up the gangplank and Erica grasped her hand to help her aboard.

"Thanks," Cathy murmured as she took in Erica's appearance. She was clad in the barest of string bikinis, two miniscule strips of cloth that showed off the most gorgeous golden tan Cathy had ever seen.

"Can I get you a drink? I just mixed a batch of Bloody Marys."

"Isn't it a bit early in the day?" Cathy asked, peering at her watch which clearly said the time was 10:45.

"Early?" Clearly, it was a question out of Erica's depth. "Oh, I see what you mean. You think there's alcohol in the drinks. Goodness, no! Perhaps I should have said they were Virgin Marys. I never drink spirits. Alcohol gives you pimples," she said, patting her flawless cheeks. "Jar...Mr. Parsons is the one who drinks the liquor. I just pretend," she stated. "That's our little secret, just between you and me. I know I can trust you not to give me away," she gurgled as she waved a long pointed fingernail under Cathy's nose.

"You can count on me," Cathy said agreeably. "Is my father in the bilges?"

"Bilges?"

"Let me put it another way. Do you happen to know where my father is at this moment?"

"Of course. He's with Jar...Mr. Parsons."

"And where is Mr. Parsons?"

"Oh, well," Erica shrugged and waved her arm. "They're somewhere aboard."

"Somehow I thought they were," Cathy said snidely, watching Erica to see what effect her tone had on the scantily clad girl. There was no reaction. Obviously, Erica had become used to having people cast her snide remarks.

"Sit down and help yourself to the sun," Erica invited as she stretched out on a brilliant orange lounge chair, her long silky legs caressing the tufted cushions.

"Thanks," Cathy muttered as she sank down onto a low deck chair. As she glanced around, Cathy knew her assessment of the luxury aboard the *Gypsy* had been underestimated. Never in her life had she seen such outspoken hedonism. It was almost scandalous. From the cockpit, where she was sitting, she could look through the glass doors leading to the salon. The floor was richly carpeted in a dark emerald green, which accented the contemporary styling of the sofa upholstery. Long plush benches surrounded the area making the focal point of the room the glass and chrome bar at the far side. The area was sky-lighted and off to one side was a winding staircase leading to the flying bridge above. Soft music flowed through the doors and also from a speaker set in a niche in the bulkhead. She imagined the entire ship was wired for the stereo system. As she watched, a white-coated steward came into the lounge from the forward section to refill the ice bucket.

"How many men make up Mr. Parsons' crew?" she asked Erica, waiting for another of the girl's vague answers.

"Three, altogether, including me," Erica answered. "You know we had to leave the engine man at Virginia Beach. Appendicitis or something."

"You mean the chief engineer, don't you?"

"I guess so. I don't pay much attention. Not to those things, anyway."

"Don't you have to use any suntan oil or sun screen?" Cathy asked, envying the girl's deep tan.

"Heavens no. My dermatologist says I have perfect skin and nothing in this world can ruin it. He said I was one of those rare people whose body actually demands the sun to stay alive. He's absolutely right." Erica squirmed and stared at Cathy. "Do you use something?"

If there was one thing she wasn't going to admit to Erica it was that she had to use baby oil and iodine to get even the faintest of color. "I'm not a sun worshipper. I prefer to while away the time under a tree with a good book."

"How boring," came the reply, as Erica turned her face a slight degree toward the sun. "I hope I don't get a tan line," she complained as she adjusted the string of her bathing suit bodice.

"Yes, I certainly hope not," Cathy agreed, noticing for the first time that Erica was completely tan, without the white marks left by any suit. It was obvious she was used to bathing in the buff.

"Tell me, Miss Marshall. What does Mr. Parsons do for a living?"

"Do?"

"Yes, do. You know. What does he do for a living? How does he support himself?"

"Oh. He sends out bills. Actually, I send them out. I'm his secretary, you know. Right now, I'm on my break."

"Amazing," Cathy cooed. "Well, I guess someone has to do it."

"I hate typing numbers. I always break my nails. Jar... Mr. Parsons is getting someone to do the numbers for me when we get back to Lighthouse Point."

Cathy was saved from further comment by the arrival of her father and Jared Parsons. Her eyes went from one to the other. Sometime during the past hour the two men had reached some sort of mutual respect for one another. Jared was wiping grease from his hands and nodding while listening to Lucas.

"You have one hell of a problem, Jared," Lucas said quietly. "Ten days, and that's only an estimate. If you have to be back in Lighthouse Point, I suggest you fly. This little beauty won't be taking to the water for some time. I'll put in a call and see what I can do about getting you that raw water pump you need and the exhaust manifold. As for the generator, you'd better bring up that one from Cape Fear. You're free to try another mechanic if you want, but if they're worth their salt, they'll tell you the same thing I did.'' Jared nodded, his features said he was resigned to Lucas' statement.

Cathy grinned when she noticed Jared glance at Erica. He looked embarrassed. Lucas was openly ogling the luscious display of satiny skin, but refrained from comment.

"Look, son," Lucas said, throwing his greasy hands around Jared's shoulder, "why don't you and Miss Marshall come by for supper tonight. Cathy can whip up some of her bisque. Won't you, Cat?" he turned to his daughter, silently pleading with her by the use of her pet name. "By then I should have some news for you from the marina. Best I can do for the moment. We eat at seven, give or take an hour or two, depending on Cat's mood."

"We'd be delighted, and you must call me Erica. Everyone calls me Erica—even Jared," the girl said sleepily from her position on the chaise. Cathy smirked and Lucas grinned at the uncomfortable expression on Jared's face.

"Yes, we'd be delighted," he replied coolly. "Dress or casual?"

"White tie," Cathy snapped irritably. "And after dinner we always go skinny dipping in the river."

"Really!" Erica squealed.

"Really," Cathy said, swinging her legs over onto the gangway, her furious eyes locking with Jared's.

"Is that a promise about the skinny dipping?" Jared asked in a husky whisper as he leaned over Cathy's descending head.

In spite of herself, Cathy laughed, her sea green eyes full of mischief. "Scout's honor. Boys on the left bank and girls on the right." Jared laughed, the sound boyish and full of fun. At that moment, Cathy felt the man go up three notches in her opinion.

Lucas gunned the outboard motor and Cathy shouted over the spurring of the engine. "That was a rotten thing you did, Dad. Now I have to spend all afternoon in the kitchen."

"That man's starved for good food and good decent people like us," Lucas shouted back. "Be charitable. A few hours of your time to make a man happy isn't asking a lot. For shame, Cathy Bissette, what kind of daughter am I raising?"

"You've already raised me and done your best! Mr. Parsons bothers me and that Miss Marshall does too. I wish you hadn't invited them. They're different from us, Dad. He's rich and she's . . . she's . . ."

"His woman," Lucas shouted extra loud to be certain Cathy heard him over the roar of the runabout.

As Lucas helped Cathy out of the boat, he put his arm around her. "Cat, don't envy her. She's what she is and you're what you are. She's the icing and you're the cake. What I'm trying to say is that you're . . ."

"I get the message, Dad, and if one more person jams the fact that I'm a real person and a homebody down my throat I'm going to get physically sick. And you don't have to patronize me, either. Stop telling me how good I am, and stop acting like a father,"

she said tartly, as she flounced up the path
that led to the house.

She couldn't remember when she'd been
so angry. She banged one pot and then another. By heaven she'd cook him a dinner
he'd never recover from. If that was all she
was good for, she would at least make sure
it was a dinner he would dream about for the
rest of his days. He could have the delicious
Erica, but she'd serve the main course, and
if she was lucky, he'd be too sated to enjoy
his platinum-haired dessert.

Cathy busied herself, her thoughts on the
dish she was about to prepare. The secret
was in the cast iron kettle, and she would die
before she divulged it to anyone. Herbs and
spices were great, but if you didn't have the
right pot all you had was herbs and spices
and fish. Hmmmmm, buttermilk biscuits
and a salad from the kitchen garden out
back. She'd also make a strawberry shortcake and just see which of the sweets Jared
Parsons preferred.

If she was going homespun, she might as
well go all the way with checkered tablecloth and napkins. A bowl of daisies from

the garden and a bottle of Scuppernong wine would do the trick. It was a pity Erica was coming to dinner, it was a perfect seduction scene. Bills! He sends out bills! Cathy shrugged and then grinned. Oh well, there were jobs and there were jobs.

Her domain in perfect order, Cathy retired to her room to ready herself for the evening, the yellow tote in her arms. Darn, she still hadn't gotten to the first paragraph of Teak Helm's galleys. Tonight for sure, the minute their company had gone, she would unroll the galleys, make herself a cup of tea, lace it with rum the way Teak Helm did, and snuggle into her nest in the high four-poster and read all night long. She knew she would live every minute of Teak's adventure right down to the last punctuation mark.

Cathy finished her leisurely bath and stepped from the tub. Wrapping a cherry colored towel around herself, she padded her way to the closet. What to wear. Her eye went to an aquamarine silk shift and then to her blue jeans, neatly folded on hangers. "What you see is what I am." Those had been her words. If she dressed up now she would definitely be suspect in Jared Parson's eyes. And that slinky dress was the one she had worn the last time she had seen Marc Hellenger. If she got dressed up her father would tease her unmercifully, and probably in front of Jared. Jared. She liked the name, it rolled off her tongue easily. It was a strong name. She finally selected a pair of designer jeans that hugged where the ads said they hugged and a daffodil colored silk shirt with a V neck. Definitely casual, her father wouldn't be the wiser. Jared would be so busy eating he wouldn't pay her the least bit of attention, so why was she fussing? She couldn't wait to see what delectable outfit Erica would wear to the *homey* little dinner party. No doubt *Vogue* had some tricky little number that cost a fortune, which Erica just *happened* to own.

A few quick swirls with the blow dryer and a quick one-two at the temples with the curling iron and she was ready. She slipped her feet into rope sandals and left the room without a second glance in the mirror. She was Cathy Bissette. She wasn't beautiful by her own standards but she would only do the best she could. I am what I am, she repeated to herself.

Bismarc was up and sniffing at the door waiting to be let out when Cathy heard the sound of the motor launch sidling up to the pier. "Oh no, Bizzy, you're staying here. We don't need another incident like this morning. Lay down now and be polite." The dog whined and made his way back to the hearth where he managed to squeeze himself between tubs of ferns and the andirons. He lay with his head on his paws, his ears cocked for the sound of a knock on the oak door. When it came, he whined again, but remained where he was.

Cathy whistled lightly when her father came in from the living room in what he called his classic golf shirt. Cathy grinned at him, then giggled. "It's wasted on me since I know you don't play golf, but Erica will never know the difference. Five dollars says she thinks it's a tennis outfit."

Lucas gave her a sheepish grin and opened the door. Her gaze went to the fourth place setting on the table and then back to Jared Parsons who stood in the doorway. Her pulse quickened as she took in his appearance.

Hmm! Cathy murmured to herself. This must be what they call separating the men from the boys. Again, she knew the casual sports outfit didn't come off a rack. Jared wore sleek white slacks and a multi-colored silk shirt. He looked loose, comfortable, poised, ready for anything. He smiled and held out a spray of greens and blossoms.

"Usually I manage something a little better than this, but it was all I could find on such short notice."

"It's a good thing none of us is allergic," Lucas drawled. "That's ragweed."

Jared shrugged. "Miss Marshall wasn't able to come and wants me to extend her apologies," he said smoothly, watching Cathy to see her reaction.

Cathy lowered her eyes, not wanting him to see the relief there, and tossed his bouquet into the trash.

"Sit down, Jared," Lucas offered. "Can I get you a drink? Brought back some of Jesse Gallagher's homemade moonshine for the occasion."

"Dad, you aren't going to give him that, are you?"

"Certainly I am. I want to see what he's made of, and what better way than to have him sample some of Jesse's finest. It's the mark of a man in these parts if you can put away half a jug."

Bismarc whined again and pawed the bricks at his feet. If there was one thing he loved it was the sight of a Jesse Gallagher jug and a few drops in his saucer.

"You take this dog here," Lucas said pointing to Bismarc. "Why, he can drink both of us under the table in sight of an hour and still get up on his feet."

"That's because he has two more feet than you do," Cathy said, enjoying Jared's close scrutiny.

"Is this serious drinking we're talking about or just a friendly toot?" Jared asked.

"Hell man, it's whatever you want it to be. We've got the whole dang night ahead of us. The only thing we have to do is eat this dinner Cat cooked for us and from then on we're on our own."

Bismarc settled himself at Jared's feet and watched him with adoring eyes. Why he could walk right out of here and take my dog with him and Bismarc would never give me a second thought, Cathy thought dismally. He was fitting in just a shade too perfectly. Here he was, sitting in her kitchen like he belonged. Drinking Jesse Gallagher's moonshine like he was born to it and carrying on an easy conversation with her father on a subject very few people knew anything about; meaning one writer named Lefty Rudder.

"You're not going to believe this, Jared, but I have every work Lefty Rudder ever wrote. That man knew everything there was to know about the sea and every manner of boat you can think of. He had a way with words that the young writers today know nothing about, with the possible exception of Teak Helm. He's about the closest to Lefty I've ever come across."

"I'm afraid I'll have to take exception to that, Lucas. I've read Rudder and Helm both and I think Teak Helm is better than Rudder. Lefty Rudder was too heavy on the narrative. You take *Sea Gray Mist* for instance. I couldn't get into that book until the fourth chapter. An author has to get your attention on the first page, the first paragraph, and that's what Helm does. He grabs you in a vice and you don't shake loose till the last paragraph. Of course, that's only my opinion."

"I couldn't agree more, Mr. Parsons," Cathy said staring at her father. Now what was he up to? He adored Teak Helm's books as much as she did.

"Can't you call me Jared like your father does? And, if it's all right with you, I'll call you Cathy." Cathy shrugged. But inside she knew anything was all right with her.

"Are you a Teak Helm fan?" she asked curiously.

"I think it's safe to say so. I've read and admired all his books. I don't have much time to read, but when I do, I'd rather read one of Helm's sea adventures than anything else. Actually, I consider it a luxury to be able to sit and read for the sheer joy of it."

"Dinner's ready," Cathy said, sitting down on the chair Jared held for her. She

ignored her father's smirk and waited for the
serving bowl to be passed to her. Everything
was perfect; the table, the food and the wine.
Not that either of the men would appreciate
the wine after Jesse's homemade concoc-
tion.

"Tell me, Cathy, what do you do? Are
you home on vacation or do you live here all
year long?"

"Me?" Cathy asked, shifting her eyes toward her father. "Why I just shrimp with my
father." Lucas reached for his wine glass as
he started to choke. "Are you all right,
Daddy?"

"Fine, fine. It just went down the wrong
way." He cast a watery glance at his daughter and shrugged. If she wanted to pretend
she was a shrimp girl, let her. Cat always had
a reason for everything she did. She was like
a dog with a bone, once it got a taste of the
marrow. He stared at Jared Parsons and said
bluntly, "It's my personal opinion that Teak
Helm has been using Lefty Rudder's work.
I told you I read all of Rudder's books and
Helm just takes the same plots and adds a
new twist here and there, and because he

writes in the first person, they're his adventures. Course I can't prove it, and I've no mind to, but it's my opinion.''

"Dad! Do you know what you're saying?" Cathy cried in outrage.

"Of course I know, and I said it was just my opinion."

Jared Parsons had stopped eating, his face was a mask of controlled fury. His voice, when he spoke, was deadly. "The opinion you just stated should never be uttered before witnesses. If I were to repeat it, it could mushroom and a man's reputation could be ruined."

"He's right, Dad. How could you say such a thing?" Cathy cried, annoyed at her father and puzzled by the vehemence in Jared's voice when he defended Teak Helm.

"Any time you've a mind to put my opinion to the test, I'll be glad to point out the similarities. I told you, I have every word Lefty Rudder ever wrote and Cat here has every book Helm ever wrote. Since no one agrees with me, it's of no matter," Lucas said, getting up from his chair. "I'll be going over to Jesse's for a while. They hooked

up his cable TV and there's a movie he invited me to see. And, Parsons, I was right
about your engine. The parts for the raw
water pump and exhaust manifold will be
here in four days, possibly five. Best I could
do. And if you want to send your crewmen
down to Cape Fear to pick up that generator you ordered, be glad to lend you my pick-
up truck. You two enjoy yourselves and save
me some of that shortcake, Cat.''

Cathy blinked, stared at Jared, her mouth
open at her father's apparent rudeness.
Jared controlled his fury and forced a grimace that Cathy supposed was to pass for a
smile. She should say something, defend her
father, but the words wouldn't come. Instead, she got up and removed the dinner
plates. ''Would you like a big piece or a little piece?'' she asked inanely.

''What?''

''Cake. Do you want a big piece or a little
piece?''

''Actually, I'd much prefer to have only
the strawberries,'' Jared replied in a tight
voice.

While Cathy spooned the strawberries into a dessert dish, she watched Jared out of the corner of her eye. Her throat was dry and her heart was fluttering like a trapped bird. "Tell me, Jared, what do you do?" she asked, striving to wipe the angry look from his face.

"I'm in sales. Supply and demand, that type of thing," he answered shortly.

"And then you send out bills," Cathy muttered as she turned to the counter for the cream.

"I'm sorry, what did you say?" he asked a frown settling on his handsome features.

"Nothing," she answered nonchalantly. "I was wondering aloud what movie Dad was going to see. How are the strawberries?"

"Delicious. And your dinner was extraordinary. I've eaten in some of the finest restaurants around the world and I can truthfully say yours was one of the best dinners I've ever eaten. Now I know why you won first prize for your recipe."

Cathy laughed. "It's the pot." Now why had she admitted that to this man? It was her closely guarded secret, the success of her She-Crab stew, and here she was babbling like a schoolgirl. Was she looking for that pat on the head from this strange man sitting beside her?

Bismarc made his way to Jared and nuzzled his leg. He backed up and stared at the man.

"I usually take him for a run along the shore about this time of day. I guess he thinks you're going to take him. He's certainly taken a liking to you." Now why was her voice so defensive?

"Then let's take him for his run," Jared said, rising from his chair. "I like to walk after dinner, something I rarely get a chance to do when I'm living aboard ship. You can clean this mess later."

"Oh, I can, can I?" Cathy sputtered. "You ate here, the least you can do is offer to help me clean up."

"That's woman's work," Jared defended coolly. "Come on, before this dog takes a fit here at my feet." He took her arm and pulled her to him. Cathy's breathing quickened at his touch and she drew in her breath. Bismarc, hearing the sound, nudged his way between Jared and Cathy, separating them, showing Jared that while he, Bismarc, might like him, Cathy was his mistress.

Dumb dog, Cathy groaned silently. When I want you to protect me I'll let you know. Jared was amused and fondled Bismarc's ear. "Clever dog you have here."

"Among other things," she said tartly, opening the door for Bismarc's wild charge. The dog waited, his eyes on Cathy. "Go ahead, Bizzy." The dog wouldn't move, he emitted a whining from deep in his throat. "Fetch me a catfish and I'll cook it for your breakfast," Cathy said, shooing the dog out the door. Bismarc needed no second urging, he was out the door like a streak.

Jared stared at Cathy. "Can he find a catfish at night in the dark water?"

"No, but he doesn't know that and it did get him out of the way."

Jared laughed, the boyish sound rippled through her. Suddenly, he took her hand in his. "I'll race you to the dock!"

"You're on!" Cathy cried, breaking loose from his hand and racing off in her long-legged stride. Midway to the dock, Jared passed her, his athletic grace evident in the way he ran with his head up and arms tucked closely at his sides.

Before she could reach the dock, he stopped and turned and she found herself running into his open arms. Laughing, she struggled for balance and it was only Jared's strong embrace that kept her from falling.

"No fair, you said to the dock."

"I changed my mind," he teased, the sound of his laughter ringing through her and tingling her toes. "Besides, I don't want to tire you out and give you an excuse for not clearing up the kitchen."

"Beast," she smiled. "You're no better than Bismarc. Eat and run," she sighed dramatically. She wished Jared would release her from his embrace. His nearness was doing odd things to her and she couldn't seem to catch her breath.

As if sensing her thoughts, he draped his arm around her shoulders and walked with her along the length of the pier. In the distance, the lights of *Sea Gypsy III* glowed through the darkness.

"It's a pity Miss Marshall couldn't come to dinner," she murmured, waiting to see if Jared would offer a further explanation of Erica's absence.

"I didn't want her to come with me and I told her so."

Cathy drew away from him and looked up into his eyes. "And are women used to doing as you say? She was extended a personal invitation, she would have been well within her rights to come to dinner, in spite of anything you said," the challenge in her voice was clear.

"Yes, I usually have my way where women are concerned," he replied, his gray eyes twinkling in response to her challenge.

"And why is that?" Cathy demanded, so angry she had to force the words from between stiff lips.

"Because I expect it," he smiled. "And also because I'm confident in my own ability to satisfy a woman in other—more pleasurable ways that make her forget my shortcomings, shall we say."

Cathy blushed vividly and was glad for the descending darkness that hid the revealing flush of color staining her cheeks. "Are you always so conceited?" she retorted, withdrawing from him until she stood precariously near the edge of the weathered planks.

"Conceited? I prefer to think of it as self-assured." A wry smile played about his lips and his eyes locked with hers and seemed to delve into her being.

Cathy could almost understand why he was so confident in himself and his effect on women. He had the handsomeness of a prince and the smile of a rogue. His broad shoulders seemed to stand between herself and the darkness, and he possessed the lean, stalking grace of a panther. She realized, to her own dismay, that she was vitally aware of his presence and of his emanating prowess. He was all that was masculine and manly, yet there was a playful hint of the boy in him. Jared Parsons would always remain young, regardless of the years he added to his age. His charm was infinite; his magnetism was boundless.

Aware that she was being drawn under his spell, Cathy tore her eyes away, eager only to put distance between herself and this overbearing man. In her haste, she came dangerously close to the edge of the dock, nearly losing her balance for the second time that night.

With the quick reflexes of a cat he snatched her away from the edge and pulled her up close against him, pressing her against his body, making her aware of the lean, hard strength he possessed.

"You see what I mean?" he said huskily, the tone of his voice sending shivers up her spine. "I simply sweep women off their feet and they fall into my arms." His mouth was close to her ear and a roaring sounded in her head. She had never been so sensitively aware of a man in her entire life.

Cathy clung to him, aware for the first time of the shock of desire that swept over her like a rising tide. "Not *this* woman," she protested, and her voice sounded unconvincing, even to her own ears. "It would take more than a plunge into the river for me to fall into your arms."

"Perhaps it would take this..."

Spellbound, she felt him move against her, watched him bend toward her. His mouth found hers and he kissed her, gently at first, then, as her traitorous body responded with a will of its own, the kiss became deeper, masterfully sensuous. His arms closed around her, molding her to the full length of his body. Her senses came alive, aware of the black sky surrounding them and the ebony waters beneath them. She was conscious of the soft, dark night and the glimmer of the bravest stars which dared to outshine the moon. The long needle pines seemed to whisper his name while the gentle sea breezes caressed and cooled their cheeks, bringing into sharp contrast the warmth of the contact between their lips.

His mouth trailed across her cheek in a caress as soft as a butterfly's wings and ignited a flame on the smooth skin just below her ear. Desire and passion licked through her veins like brushfire as she clung to him, a stirring response thundering through her that was astonishing in its intensity.

When he released her she was breathless, unable to fathom the emotions that swept through her. "You had no right to do that!" she protested hotly as his fingers wound around the base of her throat and tipped her face up to his.

"I don't think your body agrees with you," he said, his deep laugh sounding in her ears. A laugh that held all of the man and none of the boy.

Before he could capture her lips again, Cathy stumbled free of his grasp, running headlong for the river bank, knowing only that she must put distance between herself and this man who could make her pulses race and her heart pound. A man who could make her forget her principles and conspire with him for her own seduction.

She heard his footsteps pounding down the dock in hot pursuit. She heard herself squeal in dismay and was aware of a red-coated streak leaping through the trees to take a stance at the end of the dock. Bismarc set up a ferocious barking, holding Jared Parsons at bay while his mistress made her escape.

Feeling secure in the small measure of safety Bismarc allowed, Cathy turned on her heel and faced her pursuer. "Stay away from me, Jared Parsons. I know all about men like you and I have no use for your kind. Stay away! I never want to see you again!''

Jared placed his hands on his hips and leaned backward. A deep, hearty laugh that teased and mocked her with its mischief rasped against her nerves. ''That's quite impossible, *Miss Bissette*. Your father invited me to go shrimping in the morning with both of you. Needless to say, I accepted.''

Chapter Three

Always an early riser, Cathy thought this particular morning the same as the others. If her movements were a little less agile, her mind a little fuzzier, she chalked it up to the approaching storm that made itself evident through her bedroom window.

Bismarc whined at the foot of the bed. It was time to go out, and he tugged impatiently at the bedspread to show his irritation. Cathy hastily pulled on her shorts and knotted a tailored shirt at her waist. She might as well get a move on; she still had the remnants of last night's dinner to clear away before she could begin with breakfast.

She dreaded facing Lucas at the breakfast table, listening to him ramble on about his evening with Jess's cable television, and then the inevitable questions about her own evening. And she knew she wouldn't be spared his sly looks when he noted the disastrous condition of the kitchen. No one in Swan Quarter left dinner dishes sitting on the table overnight. "I think I'm living under a black cloud, Bizzy. Do you get the feeling somebody is out to get me?" The Irish setter whined impatiently, eager to be let outdoors.

On the dock, Cathy sat with her long legs drawn up to her chin, the wind whipping her light blonde hair about her face. The mist over the water swirled to the north, covering the water's surface and making it impossible to see Jared's yacht. Bismarc frolicked on the beach and soon came to join his mistress, nuzzling Cathy's hand for attention. "You know that black cloud I was telling you about? Well, I think I'd better get myself an umbrella, or I'm going to drown in the rain of my own emotions. And I don't mean from the oncoming storm, either. At least I'll be spared his company today. Dad won't be taking the trawler out with a storm coming.''

Bismarc settled himself comfortably at her side and from time to time his paws took a swipe at the low gray mist encroaching the pier. Suddenly, he growled, a low sound in his throat, and stood up, ears erect. ''He's out there, and he's watching us. That's what you're trying to tell me. He can see us, but we can't see him. He's insufferable, Bizzy. If there's one thing I know about, it's people, and there are two kinds—givers and takers. Jared Parsons is a taker. He thinks he's going to take me and add me to his collection...of women. That conceited, insufferable, arrogant, chauvinistic...'' she sputtered angrily. ''Maybe Erica what's-her-name wants to give her all to Jared Parsons, but Cathy Bissette doesn't.'' She laughed and threw her arms around the setter. ''What I'm saying is, Jared Parsons can just go fish in some other stream. And do you know something else, Bizzy? When we get back to the house, I'm going to call Dermott McIntyre and ask him if he wants to go to the Fourth of July picnic with me. I'll even let him kiss me good-night," she said defensively. "Come on, it's going to pour any minute. If we're lucky, he might get washed overboard." Bismarc howled his protest at being led back to the house.

"I cleaned up the mess you left here," Lucas Bissette grumbled as he poured his daughter a cup of coffee and set a plate of toast in front of her. "You must have had a grand evening if you couldn't clean the kitchen."

Cathy casually sipped her coffee and told her father about her evening with Jared. Suddenly, his chair settled into place with a loud thud. Lucas leaned across the table, his eyes locked with Cathy's. "For a girl who makes her living in the city of New York, and who is supposed to be as smart and intelligent as you claim to be, it just eludes me why you're making this much of a fuss over a simple little invitation."

Cathy bristled, her eyes changing to the green of emerald fire. "Most fathers," she said through clenched teeth, "would react somewhat differently if their only daughter told them a rich playboy tried to seduce her on the river bank. Or is it that you think I'm so ugly and unattractive no man would ever try something like that and you think I'm lying!"

"Women! You're just like your mother, trying to put words into my mouth." Gruffly, he touched her shoulder with his calloused hand. "No, I don't think you're ugly and unattractive, and no, I don't think you're lying. I just think you're afraid of men, Jared Parsons in particular, because he stirs something up in you and you're afraid of it. Parsons ain't the run of the mill man you've been used to. I think you might have misconstrued what happened last evening. I'm not saying Parsons isn't a playboy. He sees you as a desirable, beautiful young woman, and not the kind of woman he's used to coming in contact with. He reacted like a man; is that so terrible?"

"It's evident you're on his side. So, why don't we just drop the subject? Thanks for doing the dishes," Cathy said curtly.

"My pleasure. I'm going down to the water and check out the pier. That's a wicked wind whipping out there. What are you going to do with yourself?"

"I'm going to settle down with Teak Helm's galleys and read non-stop. On second thought, I think I'll take the pick-up and go into town and pick up a few things."

"Ah...Cat...you can't take the pick-up. I told Parsons his crewmen could use it to go up to Nags Head to see if they could get a few parts for his engine."

Cathy seethed. She'd been right the first time. It *was* a black cloud over her head, and it was getting lower by the minute. Her back stiffened as she marched from the room, Bismarc in her wake.

Cathy's anger evaporated the minute she unrolled the galleys and lost herself in the latest Helm sea adventure. It was two o'clock in the afternoon when she noticed her muscles were cramped and the sun was shining bright and clear. It had also gotten hot and muggy and she longed for a cooling swim.

Tenderly, she straightened the long galley sheets on her bed in neat order and quickly donned her swim suit, a modest two-piece affair of grass-green Lycra. Without the use of the pick-up she would have to use her old bike and pedal to her favorite inlet. Quickly, she gathered up her beach towel and a pair of thong sandals and tossed them into a bright green beach bag that matched her swim suit. At the last moment, she scooped up her portable radio and a tube of zinc oxide to protect her nose from overexposure to the sun. Packing in a slim sheaf of the galleys, she was ready to go.

Bismarc nudged her leg pointedly, pushing her toward the refrigerator. Cathy waved a bag of Oreo cookies for him to see, and he barked his approval. "To the inlet, Bizzy, and the first one in the water gets to eat the whole bag!"

Bismarc hit the water just as Cathy leaned her bike against a tall, whispering pine tree. "If you're not a chauvinist, you'll share," she said, waving the cookie bag in the air. Bismarc ignored her as he cavorted in the water.

Cathy looked around to be certain she had solitary domain of her secret place where the water was cool and calm and the sun dappled through the trees. A perfect place for skinny-dipping. She shed her two-piece suit and waded out into the water. One second there was a flash of skin and the next a mermaid broke water. Laughing happily, she played with her dog, splashing and whooping just as she had done when she was a young girl and Bismarc was a puppy.

It wasn't his words but the timber of his voice that shocked her to awareness. "Skinny-dipping, Miss Bissette?"

How had he found her? Was he spying on her, following her to finish what he'd started the night before? She tried to speak but the words wouldn't come. She nodded, her body weightless in the water. Her heart fluttered madly as she saw him standing on the river bank.

"Are you going to stay in there all day, Miss Bissette?" he asked mockingly.

Cathy found her voice. "For days, if necessary. How did you find this inlet?" she demanded, knowing he was relishing every second of her embarrassment. And to make matters worse, Bismarc had deserted her and Jared was opening her bag of cookies. He handed one to the dog and then squatted down, watching her through narrowed eyes. From time to time he nibbled on a cookie, his gray eyes laughing at her. He was going to wait her out, and when she did leave the water, she would be as wrinkled as yesterday's newspaper. He would also see the smear of zinc oxide she had smeared all over her nose. She knew his secretary never used zinc oxide. People who had perfect skin didn't need sun screens.

Bismarc daintily nosed another cookie from the bag, and in doing so the sheaf of galleys from Cathy's beach bag fell onto the washed out beach towel. Cathy watched angrily as Jared picked up the long sheets of paper and scrutinized them. "Take your hands off those!" Cathy shouted angrily. "And stop feeding my dog!" Tears stung her eyes at her predicament. "Bismarc, chase him out of here," she cried.

Jared Parsons laughed and Cathy's head reeled with the effect of the sound. "This animal well may be a champion of champions, a staunch defender of womanly virtue, plus a great bird-dog, but right now, right this minute, he's a dog who is smart enough to know who is holding the cookies." He laughed again and Bismarc sat at attention waiting to be fed his special treat. "I'd almost be willing to place a small wager that he could be trained to attack for one of these delectable morsels."

He was right. Bismarc would do anything for a cookie. "You...you..." Words failed Cathy as she sputtered, trying to tread water.

"Insufferable, unbearable, conceited, arrogant male chauvinist," Jared completed her statement and laughed, feeding Bismarc still another cookie. He stood, his hands on his hips, and grinned. "You're beginning to look a little...puckered. You better come out. And to show you what a gentleman I am, I'll turn around."

"Never!" Cathy stormed. "Sooner or later you're going to run out of cookies and then you'd better watch out, Bizzy will tear you apart."

Cathy stared at him grimly. In spite of herself, she couldn't help admiring his slim litheness, the bronze chest that stood out starkly above his tailored white shorts. How well she remembered the feel of those muscular legs pressed against her own. She had to get out of the water, trick him somehow so she could get away from him. Deliberately, she took a mouthful of water, coughing and sputtering. Instinctively, she started to flounder and gasped, "I have a cramp! Bizzy, help me!" Another mouthful of water and more coughing and sputtering. Bizzy ignored her as he chewed on a fresh Oreo. Out of the corner of her eye, as she let herself slip beneath the water, she saw Jared tense and move toward the river's edge.

From under water she could hear his legs thrashing the water as he waded out to a depth where he could swim.

Cathy had always considered herself a strong swimmer, but she was no match for Jared's powerful strokes. He had her pinned to him within seconds. Drops of water sparkled on his long, dark lushes, making her want to reach up and brush them away.

"You're a beautiful woman," Jared said huskily as his eyes devoured her hungrily.

Cathy's trembling body was not lost on Jared as he drew her closer. "You're freezing," he said softly. He laughed, "Or are you?"

Cathy struggled, fighting for escape. Her face flamed and her temper flared. Her plans had gone askew. She had intended to lure Jared into the water, and while he was swimming out to her, make her escape by heading for the shore, and at the very least, wrapping the towel around her nakedness. Now, she realized how foolish she had been to assume that Jared wasn't an excellent swimmer, as he seemed to be at everything else.

As her struggles increased, she involuntarily rose in the water, her naked torso becoming visible. One quick glance in Bismarc's direction told her she would get no help from that quarter since he had the whole bag of Oreos to himself. Jared had fed him, and now Jared was holding her and Bismarc was making no effort to help. Bismarc was not the smartest dog in the world, she decided and reluctantly stopped trying to get away.

"Have you resigned yourself to be rescued?" Jared grinned. "Admit it," he demanded, pulling her tightly against him, making her aware of his lean, hard strength and his hands holding her fast, aware of the sun glinting through the trees, the feel of the water caressing her skin. "You tricked me into the river because you didn't have the nerve to come out." There was a new note in his voice now. A throbbing note of masculinity, a teasing, sensual sound that feathered through her senses and made her feel weak.

"Admit it," he repeated against her ear, his lips caressing and finding the smooth softness near the base of her throat. "You were afraid to come for what you wanted, so you sang the song of the Lorelei and lured me in here after you." His arms became possessive, blocking out all sight and sound except the reality of his caress. His lips found hers, tasting of the slightly salty river water, cool and wet; yet, somehow, that kiss burned through her, assaulting her defenses and overpowering her protests. Mindlessly, she wrapped her arms around him, feeling his power and strength. She clung to him, weightless, buoyant, as though in a dream, and the fabric of her resistance frayed like tattered threads of flotsam and jetsam. His hands wound in her hair, his lips sought the hollow of her throat and began to trail lower.

Cathy stiffened. He thought... he actually thought... he believed she enticed him into the water to make love to her! Crack! She brought up her hand and at the same time kicked her legs, pushing him off balance. She dove, clean and deep, surfacing as far away from him as she could get. She was tired and she knew she could never reach the river bank before him if he decided to pursue her. A backward glance told her he was doing exactly that, a murderous glint in his eyes. She still had some fight left in her, and would go down fighting if she must. "You stay away from me," she gasped, taking an unintentional mouthful of water. Jared was upon her, holding her head above water with one hand, the other was locked about her waist. Tears scalded Cathy's eyes as she realized what was to come. "Please," she begged, "let me go! I didn't...I only wanted to get away from you. I didn't mean for this. Let me go."

Jared frowned, noticing the tears in her eyes. She couldn't be...not in this day and age! A virgin!

Cathy stared into his gray eyes and knew immediately what he was thinking. She felt ashamed, prudish, like a little girl all rolled into one. Then she became angry, defending herself against his silent mockery. "Yes, I'm a virgin, and I intend to remain that way until the day I get married. If that makes me hokey or cornball in your eyes, then so be it. You see, Mr. Parsons," she said, making his name sound like a disease, "I can handle my decision. It must come as a shock to you to find there's at least *one* female who can resist your charms. And I'm her!"

She turned and struck out for the river bank with sure, even strokes, belying the fact that her heart was pounding and her breathing was ragged.

Jared didn't follow, but she felt his eyes stinging her. She watched him from the shore as she stepped into the bottom of her swim suit and then knotted the top securely. She gathered her belongings and stood a moment, staring at Jared as he treaded water exactly where she had escaped him. With four cookies still to go in the cellophane bag, Bismarc yelped in outrage as Cathy climbed onto her bike and pedaled away. Dejectedly, he followed the wobbling bicycle, hoping for a stray crumb along the way.

Even though Cathy knew she wasn't being followed by Jared, she pedaled furiously, skirting rocks strewn along the path. At the last moment, before turning into the road which led to her house, she decided to ride into the village and get the few things she needed from the drugstore. Just in case, she told herself, Jared Parsons took it into his head to follow her home.

Cathy kept her pace an easy one for Bismarc to follow. The ride to the center of Swan Quarter's business district was less than a mile, and Bismarc kept an easy lope beside her. Her circuit took her past the ferry boat landing which all summer long took happy tourists out to the island of Ocracoke, where some say the infamous pirate, Blackbeard, buried his treasure. The ferry landing was quiet now, and she followed the road to the center of the tiny town.

"Wait here, Bizzy," she instructed as she leaned her bike outside the corner drugstore, "and don't chase any little old ladies. Be a good dog and I'll get some more cookies," Cathy said, trying to bribe the dog. If there was one thing he loved, it was padding after little old ladies and snouting against their shopping bags.

Her purchases secure in her beach bag, Cathy mounted her bicycle and made her way down the quiet village street. She glanced up at the sun and estimated the time. She had spent much longer than she had anticipated talking to Mr. Gruber, the druggist, and his wife, who insisted she have a root beer float and tell her all about New York City. Cathy almost missed his tall figure, but there was no way she could have missed Erica's striking good looks in her colorful shorts and T-shirt. "Hide, Bizzy," she hissed as she skirted into the nearest alleyway, almost toppling from her bike.

In the shadows of the alleyway, between the grocer's and the hardware store, Cathy could hear the click of Erica's high heeled shoes on the pavement and recognized the deep timber of Jared's voice. They were heading her way! How had Jared and Erica arrived in town so quickly, she wondered. Then she remembered his runabout and the public dock. He had left the inlet and gone back to his yacht, picked up Erica and had come into town. The public dock was only a block away from the village.

Cathy felt her heart sink. By the sound of their voices, they were heading right for her. If they should notice her hiding like a criminal in the alley, she would appear more foolish than ever. What was happening to her? Here she was, a full grown woman, hiding!

"If you have something to say, Erica, say it!" Jared demanded. His tone was a far cry from the amused tone he always used with Cathy. Jared was angry, angrier than she knew he was capable of being.

Erica stopped just at the end of the alley where she turned on her incredibly high heels to face Jared. "Very well, I'll say it! I don't like the way you look at that little goody two shoes. I may be what I am, but I've never been a liar. And last, but not least, I'm not dumb and I have *no* intention of continuing the role you want me to play. A secretary is one thing, but don't expect me to play the blithering idiot. Your little swamp girl is no fool. Remember when she came out to the yacht? Well, the first thing she asked was what you did for a living. I played my part to the hilt, and believe me when I tell you, she didn't buy it. Not one word of it."

Cathy, hiding in the shadows, saw Jared tense and his eyes narrow.

"What did you tell her?"

"I told her you sent out bills. Let her figure it out. If I'm supposed to be brainless," Erica complained, "it was the perfect answer." Her strident voice lowered and she moved a step closer to Jared. "Something's wrong, Jared. Something has come between us. Tell me not to worry, lie to me if you must," she pleaded. Seeing no response, she spat angrily. "It's Pollyanna, isn't it? You like that girl and all her homey talents. What do you suppose she'd be like in bed? She's shaped like a plank! Or haven't you gotten that far in your thinking? If you never believe anything else, believe this. That one is holding out for a ring and a marriage contract."

Cathy's face flamed and she was certain they could see it shining like a beacon from the dark alleyway. An anger which she'd never known she was capable of raced through her and stiffened her back. How dare they talk about her this way? A plank, indeed!

"That's enough Erica. You know no more about the girl than I do, and if there's one thing I don't do, have never done, it's seducing sixteen-year-old girls."

"Sixteen!" Erica laughed shrilly. "Sixteen! Try adding eight or nine years onto that number and you'll have her age. She may look sixteen to you, but she isn't."

Cathy, from her hiding place, almost cried aloud in outrage. Sixteen! Even after this afternoon, when he had held her in his arms, kissed her, he thought she was sixteen! Her blue-green eyes ignited into fires. He had seen her naked, had watched her pull on her bathing suit. And still he thought she was sixteen! Cathy nearly moaned aloud with humiliation. She knew she was slender, but she had never thought of herself as being built like a plank nor of seeming underdeveloped. *Sixteen!*

Erica advanced a step toward Jared and wrapped her arms around his neck. "I'm bored, Jared. Can't you hurry Lucas so we can leave this place?" Her long nails trailed the soft hair at the nape of his neck. "Let's hurry back to the yacht," she whispered, and the hushed tone echoed through the alley. "I'm feeling lonely and I want you to do something about it . . . soon, very soon."

Cathy couldn't bear another moment of seeing them, hearing Erica's soft purr as she made her unabashed invitation to Jared. Couldn't bear to see the woman's long, painted nails trailing through Jared's hair, just as her own fingers had done hours earlier when he had swam out to her and held her in his arms and created an earthshattering stir of her emotions. With a silent cry, Cathy buried her face in her hands and only knew that an eternity later, when she at last was able to lift her head, both Erica and Jared were gone.

Back in her room, Cathy tossed her beach bag and her purchases from the drugstore onto the bed. She removed the slim sheaf of Teak Helm's galleys and dropped them beside the sheets she had already read.

The house was quiet, disturbingly so. She didn't want to be alone with her thoughts; she didn't want to remember that scenario she had witnessed from the alleyway. She felt besmirched and foolish because of Jared Parsons, and stupidly chagrined to be betrayed by her own dog. "You," she accused Bismarc as he nosed hungrily at the zipper on her beach bag, "would sell your soul to the devil for an Oreo cookie." The setter whined pitifully at her stern words. "You actually sat there stuffing yourself while I made a fool of myself, naked as the day I was born. I actually came out and said I was saving myself, and I admitted I was a virgin to that... that man! Now I'm going to have to face him on the trawler in the morning when we leave to go shrimping. How can I look at him knowing he thinks I'm . . . I'm . . . sixteen! I hate him! And you can just get out of my sight too, you . . . dog!'' Cathy cried brokenly as she threw herself on the bed, crushing the galleys into a heap. At first she fought the tears but then gave in. She hiccoughed and sobbed, all the while beating the pillow with clenched fists. Cautiously, Bismarc poked his head around the door frame, then slinked his way to the bed. Cathy was asleep, the tears drying on her cheeks. He whined and tried to lick her hand, but gave up when she pulled away. Disheartened at this lack of attention, he left the room, but not before he managed to nose the package of cookies out of the beach bag.

Chapter Four

Through most of the night Cathy prayed for rain. The last thing in this world that she wanted to do was to spend the day on a small trawler with Jared Parsons and his "secretary."

But the heavens chose not to comply with her prayers and produced perfect shrimping weather. The sun was already making the promise of a beautiful day as it shed a red-gold haze on the horizon. A fine smoke mist was dissipating off the water, and there was just enough breeze to sway the highest tops of the tall pines. Drat!

As Cathy rose from her bed, Bismarc was already demanding to be let out. "Calm down, Bizzy, let a girl get her eyes open, will you?" Bismarc barked anxiously. "All right, all right, I'm hurrying!"

Hastily, she stripped off her light blue baby doll pajamas and pulled on her two-piece bathing suit, covering it with jeans and a T-shirt. "Do you think I can have a chance to brush my teeth, if I hurry?"

Carrying her Topsiders in her hand, she ran with Bizzy out the kitchen door and down to the dock. The early morning dew was cool on her bare feet, and the sun was higher on the horizon, spreading its golds and coloring the landscape. Before she even reached the dock, she could hear the powerful motor of Jared's motor launch breaking the stillness. Her heart sank. Since she hadn't succeeded in her wish for bad weather, she had begun to hope that he and Erica had overslept and that she and Lucas could slip out on the trawler without them.

Bizzy set up a rousing welcome, long before the runabout docked.

Jared threw the bowline with perfect aim, lassoing the piling and securing the boat. He spotted her and waved. "Coffee ready?" he called.

Cathy immediately bristled. Of all the insufferable...There sat Erica in the stern seat, looking as though she'd just stepped from the pages of *Women's Wear Daily,* and he was asking *her* if she had coffee ready! She knew his crew was still securing the new engine for the yacht, and so that left Jared and Erica alone on board; still, if Erica couldn't even make a pot of coffee what *did* she do? Cathy gulped, her face reddened. She didn't want to think about what Erica did for Jared.

"Hey, are you still sleeping? I asked you if you'd made coffee? Didn't you hear?"

"I heard," Cathy answered from between clenched teeth. "I knew Dad had invited you to come trawling with us; I didn't know he'd also invited you to breakfast."

"He didn't," Jared smiled an infuriating smile, "I only asked if you'd made coffee."

He turned to help Erica onto the dock, warning Bizzy in a gentle command to stay away.

Cathy watched Bizzy, a russet red form of eager impatience, sit down and control himself from rushing onto the pier and running to Jared. She eyed Erica's short shorts of yellow terry cloth and her skimpy white top which left little to the imagination. Cathy couldn't help but smile. Even Erica's "perfect skin" would show the effect of a long day on the trawler, with the burning sun reflecting off the water and with nowhere to take shelter but the cramped wheelhouse.

"Lucas up and about?" Jared asked conversationally.

"I suppose so. I haven't seen him yet this morning, but he's more than likely bringing the trawler around from the marina." Cathy turned on her heel, slapping her side in a silent call to Bismarc who was affectionately hugging Jared's thigh.

"Where're you going?"

"You seem to be dying for a cup of coffee. I'm going to the house to make it. Also, I've got to make the lunches for today. Hard work makes for big appetites, and there's no place on a trawler for anyone who doesn't intend to do his day's share of work." She looked pointedly at Erica who didn't seem to notice.

"Don't worry about the lunches," Jared said. "Erica whipped something up in the galley." He jumped back into the runabout and hefted out a wicker basket.

Cathy eyed the basket suspiciously and shrugged, saying nothing. Probably green molded bologna sandwiches and yogurt.

Jared and Erica sat at the kitchen table drinking coffee while Cathy busied herself. "What are you doing?" Jared asked between sips of hot coffee.

"Making lunch."

"I've already told you Erica whipped something up in the galley...."

"Then let me put it this way. I'm making *my* lunch. When I work, I get hungry. It's as simple as that." Cathy felt his eyes on her every move, making her self-conscious. The butter knife, thick with peanut butter, slipped from her fingers and clattered to the floor. She couldn't seem to control her shaking hands and the hot coffee which she was pouring into a thermos slopped over the sides, making a brown puddle on the shiny counter top. The hard-boiled eggs she had prepared the day before crunched to the floor, and even the apple she packed into the brown paper bag rolled out of her reach.

"That's quite an act you've got there, Miss Bissette. What do you do for an encore?" There was humor in his eyes, but his tone was dead pan.

Choking back a snarl, Cathy wrestled the peanut butter knife away from Bismarc. "I think I hear the trawler," she remarked as a low put-put of a marine engine came to her ears. "If you're ready, let's go."

Erica, who had been silent since arriving, stood and brought her coffee mug to the sink. Jared brought his too, but at least he rinsed it under the running tap and turned it upside down in the dish drainer. Cathy sniffed. If Erica's lack of housekeeping instincts was any indication of the lunch, Cathy was glad to have the cracked hard-boiled eggs and gooey peanut butter and jelly sandwich. "Come on, Bizzy. Dad's here and rarin' to go."

"You're not bringing that...that dog, are you?" Erica asked, her expression clearly indicating her concern.

"Of course we are," Cathy snapped. "Bizzy always comes with us, don't you, boy?" She patted Bismarc's head. "He'd be heartbroken if we left him home. C'mon, boy, Dad's waiting." She pointedly stood by the back door, holding it open for Bizzy and Jared and Erica.

Lucas waved from the bow of the trawler then went back to stringing line through the winches which would haul the heavy nets out of the water.

Jared ran ahead carrying the wicker basket, Bizzy barking at his heels. "Can I give you a hand there, Luke?" he called.

Cathy watched Jared's easy movements, admiring, in spite of herself, his athlete's grace. Erica was having a difficult time making her way across the expansive lawn in her spike heeled sandals. "Dad's not going to let you on board wearing those things," she said, motioning toward Erica's shoes.

"They're not safe, and they're murder on the decks."

"Oh, I won't wear them on board. I'll take them off."

"Erica, I suppose I should warn you. The decks of the trawler aren't plushly carpeted like they are on the yacht. And bare feet are treacherous on wet decks. Don't you have a pair of Topsiders like these?"

"You mean those sneakers?" Erica curled her lip in distaste.

"They're not sneakers. They're deck shoes." She stopped and showed her the bottom of the shoe. "See, the grooves on the rubber sole act like little squeegies, even on a wet deck."

"Oh. Is that what they do?" Erica sneered, obviously disinterested, indicating that she wouldn't be caught dead wearing sneakers unless she was on a tennis court.

"Suit yourself," Cathy called, running ahead and leaving Erica to hobble down the grassy slope to the pier.

While the pulleys and lines did most of the hard labor of lifting the heavy nets out of the water, it was still a tedious and backbreak-

ing job to empty the funnel-shaped nets and
sort through, separating the assortment of
fish, crabs' debris and the prized shrimp.
Over and over again, when the lines became
taut and dragged to the bottom, the winches
were manned and creakily hoisted the nets to
the decks of the trawler.

Erica issued shrill little shrieks whenever
a fish bounced out of the net and flopped
around the deck, and she turned up her nose
at the sight of the shrimp, with their ugly little heads and thread-like little legs. But it was
the crabs that were her undoing. Fierce and
warlike, they battled with each other in the
tall plastic cans, and Cathy couldn't resist
pretending to accidentally drop a few of
them onto the slick, water-puddled deck.
Claws raised in self-defense, skittering in
their peculiar sideways motions, their dark
olive bodies raised up over their pale blue
legs, they sought the shadowy recesses of the
boat. Unable to control herself, Erica
screamed, demanding that something be
done before those monsters chewed off the
tips of her little pink toes.

In her panic, Erica sought safety next to Jared, but before she could reach him, her bare feet slipped on the wet deck, and she went tumbling down.

Lucas turned to help her stand on her feet. "Watch out there, little lady," he said softly. "Bare feet and a wet deck are dangerous. You could go overboard." Erica smiled beguilingly up at Lucas, fully aware of her power over the weaker sex. Lucas cleared his throat. "Cat, why don't you lend your Topsiders to Erica? You're a lot more familiar with this boat than she is. What do you say?"

Cathy was beyond words. Her own father! For her answer, she glared at him. Sure, give over her own shoes to Erica, and she could take her chances barefoot. Grudgingly, seeing the plea in Lucas' eyes, she kicked off her shoes and tossed them at Erica.

She went back to work at the stern of the boat, her tasks taking her close to Jared. "That was very nice of you, Cathy. Erica's never been on a work boat before. I guess she didn't know what to expect or how to dress. Part of the blame is mine, I didn't even notice what she was wearing.''

Biting remarks died in Cathy's throat. He hadn't noticed what the beautiful Erica was wearing! She supposed it just went to prove that any man could become impervious to a woman's charms when they were so blatantly offered. Besides, after praising her on her generosity, how could she tell him how deeply she resented giving over her Topsiders? She didn't like Erica and she didn't like sharing her possessions with her.

Some of Cathy's bitterness at having to spend the day working the trawler with Jared Parsons melted away. She began to take notice of him as he worked the lines. He was skillful at everything he did, Cathy thought; but, somehow, in the back of her mind, she suspected that Jared was no stranger to hard work. Something about the way he used his hands when working the lines, and the way his muscles bunched in his bronzed back when he made the hoist, let her know that Jared hadn't always lived the easy life of a playboy.

As she worked beside him, they set about an easy pace, matching one another's rhythm in a harmonious determination to get the job done. From time to time she caught Jared looking at her and she knew it was with wonderment and appreciation that she could put in a hard day's work.

"We work well together. Have you noticed?" His voice was warm, friendly. And was she wrong? Had she detected a note of admiration? So Jared Parsons' interests didn't only lay in long-limbed, beautiful women who whiled away their days soaking up the sun and watching their fingernails grow. With renewed vigor, Cathy put her back into her work, liking the nearness of this tall, sun-bronzed man whose eyes could flash with something that could make her heart pound and her pulses race.

Lucas stepped out of the wheelhouse, his expression complimenting his crew on a good morning's work. "I was thinking of making a heading for Indian Island. We could have lunch and then head into Belhaven and see what we get for our catch."

* * *

Under the tall trees on the isolated island, the shade was cool and the breeze refreshing. Jared waded ashore with the wicker basket Erica had packed, and Cathy followed, careful to keep her little brown paper bag out of the water. Bizzy leaped over the side and followed them.

Erica, now fully aware of crabs in their active state, refused to follow. With an indulgent smile Jared went back and carried Erica ashore.

"What have you got there, Cat?" Lucas asked, questioning the brown paper bag.

"My lunch."

"But that's a pretty heavy basket Erica packed...."

"No thanks, green bologna sandwiches and yogurt aren't my thing. Bizzy and I will share what I've got here."

Dropping down onto the sand, Cathy opened her lunch and pulled out her sandwich. She opened her thermos and poured herself coffee and was about to offer some to Lucas just as Erica opened the lunch basket. Jared spread a bright, checkered cloth and proceeded to help Erica empty the basket. Wine, cheeses, Beluga Caviar, assorted crackers, potted meats...a feast for kings!

"Sure you won't join us, Cat? This here is some spread Erica packed for us." The twinkle in Lucas' eyes challenged her, daring her to toss her meager peanut butter sandwich aside and join them in devouring all the goodies Erica had thought to bring.

"No thanks, that's a little too rich for my blood. Bizzy and I will...Bizzy! You come back here!" Too late. Cathy watched as her dog nosed around Lucas and Jared, begging for pieces of cheese and even lapping up a cracker spread with caviar. He was gobbling it down like he was born to gourmet goodies instead of dog food.

Cathy had never been so glad to get back on board as she was when they finished their lunch. It had been a long day, and it was going to be even longer before they got home late that evening. They had made surprisingly good time from Swan Quarter all the way up river to Belhaven, but it was still a long way home. She had humiliated herself at lunch. She had tried to make a fool of Erica, expecting the worst, and she had made a fool of herself. It was obvious to everyone, even to Bizzy, that her little sandwich couldn't compare with what Erica had brought. Why couldn't she have been gracious and accepted the lunch? Why was she so stubborn?

They trawled the nets eastward to the mouth of the Pungo River where they would swing into Belhaven. It was nearly four in the afternoon, and they would just make it to the fish wholesaler where they would sell their day's catch.

Lucas was excited by the size of their catch, praising Jared and promising to work extra duty in getting the yacht seaworthy.

The decks were slick with fish oil and water, and Cathy was finding it more and more difficult to keep her footing. She cast a murderous glance in Erica's direction and saw that she was sitting in the shade of the wheelhouse, her feet propped up on the bulkhead. And on her idle feet were the Topsiders.

Her anger worked its way down to her fingers, and Cathy found it increasingly dif-

ficult to work the lines. She had been leaning over the rail when Erica came up behind
her, startling her. Her bare foot slipped, her
arms reached out, her fingers clutching at
the lines. Quicker than the blink of an eye,
Cathy went over the side and was underwa-
ter, sputtering and choking with shock. By
the time she pushed herself to the surface,
the trawler was more than fifty feet away.
She could see her father's anxiety in the set
of his shoulders and the way he was pointing. Jared was poised on the starboard rail,
jumping feet first into the river.

"Oh, no," Cathy wailed. She was perfectly capable of swimming to the boat. Why
did Jared think he had to save her? The last
thing in this world Cathy wanted was to have
Jared Parsons take credit for rescuing her.

Her arms stroked through the water, her
legs stretched out and kicking, propelling her
forward. But Jared had already left the boat
and was swimming in long powerful strokes
toward her. Twice in one week! It was too
much! She was aware that Lucas had cut the
motor on the trawler, and he and Erica were
leaning over the side watching. She could

have made it to the side of the boat within minutes. Even Bizzy seemed to know she was in no danger. She heard him barking and saw the russet streak as he plunged in over the side. He thought she was playing, and he had made up his canine mind to join her.

Jared swam toward her, meeting her halfway. "Go back. I'm all right, I don't need your help."

"This is the second time you've cried 'wolf,' Miss Bissette, and I think it's time you had a spanking. And I'm just the man to do it!"

She saw that he was suddenly angry, all concern for her leaving his face. He thought she purposely fell overboard to get him into the water to save her. She remembered the last time he jumped into the river, when she had pretended to be in trouble so she could get ashore and into her clothes. Cathy's face burned with embarrassment. There was no use in trying to explain to this insufferable, arrogant man. She swam away from him, her efforts taking her in the direction of the trawler.

"Did you hear what I said? I said you deserve a spanking."

"I heard. And what makes you think you're man enough," she sputtered.

Instead of an answer, he swam, overtaking her. "This makes me think I'm man enough." He reached for her, his fingers gripping her shoulders. She felt him pushing her down, down, under the water's surface. He dove, holding her against him, overpowering her struggles. His embrace was intimate, molding her body against his. Beneath the waters of the Pamlico, his mouth found hers, crushing her lips with his own, quelling her protests.

In spite of herself, Cathy wrapped her arms around his neck; her lips answered his kiss. She felt herself floating into a world of sensuality she had never known existed, until Jared Parsons led her through the portholes to a place where passions lay just beneath the surface and desire was a food for the soul.

Breaking surface, Cathy gasped, swallowing air. His hands were on her tiny waist, holding her firmly, refusing to release her.

The sunlight sparkled off the droplets of water that tipped his dark lashes. He smiled at her and there was no hint of mockery to be found there.

"Everything okay?" they heard the call from the trawler. Jared waved and made the three ring sign, but his eyes never left her face, and they seemed to linger on her mouth. Cathy felt herself flush.

"We'd better get back," she said softly.

"Yes, we'd better," he answered, but regret was there in his eyes and in the husky sound of his voice.

Cathy felt herself thrill to the emotions Jared could arouse in her. She wanted him to drag her beneath the surface again, and to feel the pressure of his mouth against hers, to feel herself a prisoner of his arms and mistress of his desires.

Bizzy's arrival broke her out of her thoughts. And they swam back to the trawler, Bismarc following closely behind.

The sun was setting low in the west, and darkness was falling over the river. Lucas snapped on the trawler's running lights and left Jared at the helm in the wheelhouse. The night was soft and warm; the breezes from the motion of the boat were gentle and the sounds of the engines were monotonous yet somehow soothing. The door to the wheelhouse was left open so Jared could join in the conversation out on the stern deck. Lucas was triumphant over the price the day's catch had brought; and, as always, when in a particularly jovial mood, he became loquacious, this time bending Erica's ear.

"Yes sir, lived my whole life on this river. I still love it. It's God's country. It's not the boondocks, either. Some pretty important people have pulled into these parts. Take Lefty Rudder, for instance."

Cathy sat on the cooler, sipping coffee. She smiled when she heard Lucas mention Lefty Rudder. She knew he would go on and on about the famous author until they pulled into Swan Quarter, a good two hours away.

Erica looked questioningly at Lucas. "You know Lefty Rudder?"

"Do I know him? Why he was just about the best friend a man could have. Course we were both young men when I knew him.

He'd just started his writing career. But he was a good man, the salt of the earth.''

Cathy noticed that Jared, in the wheelhouse, was paying rapt attention to this conversation. He visibly cocked an ear while his gaze was focused ahead as he took the boat down the river.

Erica spoke again, her voice denoting her incredulity. "If you were such a good friend of Lefty Rudder's, then you must know that Jared..."

Jared Parsons swung around, his eyes dark and warning. His abrupt movement caught Erica's notice, and her words were cut off. Cathy watched with curiosity. What had Erica been about to say about Jared and the venerated Lefty Rudder that he hadn't wanted her to reveal?

Lucas turned to look at Jared, and there was a devilish glint in his eye. Whatever the secret was, Cathy knew her father was aware of it. It seemed everybody knew—everyone except Cathy, but she was determined not to ask any of them what was going on.

Chapter Five

Cathy seethed inwardly as she banged the copper pots on her kitchen. Her pretty features were tight and grim, knowing her father was grinning behind her back. "Why don't you say it? I know exactly what you're thinking and you're wrong. I did not, I repeat, I did *not* stumble and fall off the boat on purpose so Jared Parsons could save me. I've never fallen off a boat in my life and you know it!" Hands on her hips, she glared menacingly at her father. "Erica startled me and I lost my footing."

"Simmer down and get on with your cooking. You have to be at the judging booth by three o'clock and that doesn't give you much time," Lucas drawled. "Tell me, are you going to enter any of the other contests?" Lucas asked, hoping to side-track his daughter onto a more pleasant subject.

Cathy tossed the crab meat into the large copper pot, wishing it were Jared Parsons she was adding to the boiling water. She couldn't dwell on the handsome man any longer nor his beautiful companion; she had to concentrate on what she was doing or she would never win first prize or any other prize for that matter. "I'm entering the disco contest with Dermott McIntyre."

"You're what?" Lucas exploded. "Dermott has two left feet and a mind to match." His tone turned fatherly as he patted Cathy on the shoulder. "Look, why don't we sit down here and have a little father-daughter chat. You're going about this all wrong," he said, not bothering to wait for her reply. "In my day, when a young woman wanted to snare a man, she did it...subtly. You've been acting like a goat in a field of orchids. You take your mother now. She caught me with the oldest trick in the book. She let me think I was doing the pursuing while she was actually manipulating me like a puppet. She never moved off that swing on her front porch. A wink and a little show of leg and I was hooked. She didn't go falling off any boat or get caught skinny dipping. You young people!'' he said disgustedly.

"That does it!'' Cathy stormed, banging her spoon on the side of the stove. "I'm going back to New York!''

"Quitter. Only cowards quit when the going gets tough. Cut and run. What are you afraid of?'' Lucas demanded as he stuffed his pipe with fragrant tobacco. His pipe drawing to his satisfaction, Lucas continued, "If you leave now, you'll be playing right into Miss Erica's hands.''

"You still don't understand, do you? I don't *want* Jared Parsons. I don't *need* Jared Parsons! Also, I would appreciate it, Dad, if you would refrain from mentioning his name to me again. I'll handle this in my own way without any help from you.'' Tears burned Cathy's eyes, and she felt her hand tremble

as she stirred the bubbling contents in the
copper pot. Jared Parsons had made a fool
of her. How was she going to look at him
and not remember what he had said about
looking like sixteen? She was going to handle it all right. Lucas was right, going back
to New York wouldn't solve anything. She
was what she *was*. There was no way she
could even begin to compare herself to the
ravishing Erica. At that moment, she would
have given her back teeth if she could make
Jared Parsons' eyes light up. She was at-
tracted to him, but that was her secret. And
if she responded to his kisses, that was her
secret, too. If her body ached, no one would
know but herself. Jared Parsons would never
know that. Life does go on, she thought bitterly. Grandpa Bissette had always said when
there was nowhere else to turn and nowhere
to go, you simply pulled up your socks and
started all over in another direction. Cathy
looked down at her feet and giggled. She
bent over and gave her tennis socks a tug and
winked at her father. He nodded through a
cloud of fragrant smoke from his pipe.

The She-Crab stew bubbling to her satisfaction, Cathy withdrew to her bedroom and began to straighten it up. Carefully, she folded the Teak Helm galleys into a neat pile and stood staring down at the fine print. Did she dare call her boss back in New York and tell him how disappointing the manuscript was? The Teak Helm fans would know immediately that this novel wasn't up to par. He could be ruined. How had it gotten as far as galley form? Why hadn't someone asked for a rewrite? A first year journalism major could see what needed to be done. Her cardinal rule had always been—never dupe a reader who has spent his hard-earned money to buy a book—and Teak Helm was very close to duping his fans. Cathy sighed. There was nothing she could do. She wasn't Teak Helm's editor and had little to say in the matter. Too many characters, too many inconsistencies to make the novel work. She slid the long strips of paper into her dresser drawer. She felt betrayed, angry, that a writer she didn't know but loved had disappointed her. The reviews would be horrendous. Well, it wasn't her problem, and she had to get on with the day.

The apricot-scented bubble bath was so inviting Cathy slid down into the slippery water and leaned back, relaxing her muscles slowly. She hadn't realized how tense she was. Come to think of it, she had been overwrought ever since she first set eyes on Jared Parsons. How could a man, a man she knew nothing about, have this effect on her? Why did she tremble and her heart beat so fast when he was near or when she thought of him as she was doing now? No one had ever kissed her the way Jared Parsons kissed her. She flushed when she remembered how she felt with her naked breasts pressed against him. The alien ache and emptiness was back. She squirmed in the steamy wetness and forced her mind to think of Dermott and the coming disco contest. Just once she would like to win something besides a homemaker award. She was a good dancer. If she was lucky, Dermott's left feet would sprout wings at the eleventh hour and they would win the contest. It would be a fun night, regardless if she won the contest or not. The Fourth of July Fair was the biggest event of the year in Swan Quarter. She had always looked forward to the event and in years past enjoyed each and every contest. Jared Parsons would be there, thanks to her father's gracious invitation. She was going early, ahead of her father, so she would be spared sitting next to Jared and Erica. With her luck, she would spill her stew under Jared's gaze, and Erica would cluck her tongue, and she would be reduced to tears and make a fool of herself once more.

Cathy stepped from the tub and slipped into her robe. Bismarc whined and scratched at the door, forcing her thoughts back to the present. "Just a minute, boy." She bent over the tub and wiped up the excess water and then hung the towel neatly on the rack. She looked around the small bathroom and was satisfied that she was leaving it the way she found it—neat and clean. Besides being a country girl, she was clean and neat. Qualities that would certainly endear any man to her. "Ha!" she snorted, opening the door and fending off Bismarc. "Let's face it, Bizzy, I am plain and neat. Tidy, if you like that word better. And I'm dull. I blush when a man looks at me, and I get nervous if a man kisses me. No, that's not quite true, I get nervous and weak in the knees when Jared Parsons looks at me and kisses me, there's a difference." Bismarc cocked his head to the side and growled deep in his throat. It was evident to Cathy that the Irish Setter didn't care for her self-pitying tone. She tweaked his ears and chased him from the room. Bismarc took it as a sign that she wanted to play and leaped on the bed. Cathy dived for him and they tussled on the bed, Bizzy with his teeth pulling at her terry robe. Laughing and tugging at the belt, Cathy fell backward. Bismarc relaxed his grip on her robe and growled, his ears straight, his tail still.

"I do seem to find you in the oddest situations, Miss Bissette. I apologize for intruding on your frolicking, but your father said I would find you up here reading. He needs the boat key, and he thought you might have it." He grinned down at her, enjoying the swell of her creamy breasts which were spilling from the loose robe and the long expanse of thigh that was visible. Cathy blinked and then clenched her teeth. "There should be a law that prohibits men like you from . . . from entering women's bedrooms. I don't have the key, and if I did, I wouldn't give it to you." Now, why had she said that? She scrambled off the bed and tied the belt so tight she had to catch her breath.

"Your father seemed quite positive that you had the boat key. He said he saw you drop it in your carry-all." Before she had a chance to reply, Jared had the yellow bag in his hand and was extracting the second half of Teak Helm's galleys from the depths. For someone who was interested in a key, he certainly was scrutinizing the printed pages in his hand. He said nothing, laying the rolled pages on the pine dresser. He fumbled in the depths of the bag and withdrew a shiny silver key. "Somehow, Miss Bissette, I didn't think you capable of a lie," he said coolly, his eyes narrowed as he stared at her.

"I'm not," Cathy said shortly. "Dad must have put the key in there himself. Now, if you'll kindly get out of my room, I'd like to dress."

Jared Parsons' tone was cool and mocking when he spoke. "For some strange reason I get the impression you don't like me very much." His eyes darkened as they narrowed to mere slits, making Cathy draw in her breath. "I find that strange, especially since I took my life in my hands to save you on two separate occasions. One would think that you would be...grateful to say the least."

He was doing it to her again, and she was allowing it. How many times was she going to make a fool of herself in front of him? She should be saying something, anything, to make herself look less like a ninny. The words stuck in her throat as she stared at him. Let him think whatever he wanted, she thought rebelliously. He was staring at her differently. Her breath caught in her throat and her pulse hammered. She took a step backward and then another. Panic coursed through her when she remembered she wore nothing beneath the terry robe. Her eyes raked the room, coming to rest on Bismarc who was busy licking Jared's tennis shoe. She swallowed hard and backed still further away from the man in front of her who was making no move to do anything beside scratch Bismarc's ears. He laughed. "Relax, Cathy. I'm not after your virtue. When I decide to make love to a woman, it's usually a mutual decision. And," he said, laughing again, "this is hardly the time or the place." His voice sobered as his stare locked with hers. "I've never attacked a woman yet. You're safe." His voice was cold now, the words clipped like chips of ice. "Thank you for the key, and I apologize for disturbing you."

Cathy all but fell on the bed, a sob catching in her throat. Did she hear his muttered words right as he walked through the door? Had he really said, "There will be another time and another place," or was that what she wanted to hear? "I can't handle this," she cried over and over. "Come here,

Bizzy,'' she said, longing for the comfort of the dog's warm body. She needed something to wrap her arms around. ''Bizzy!'' Cathy sat up on the bed and sniffed as she dabbed at her eyes. The unmitigated gall of the man. He stole her dog. ''Dognapper,'' she shouted angrily.

Chapter Six

Cathy graciously accepted the blue ribbon for her She-Crab stew and smiled winningly at the judges and then at her father who was beaming proudly. Jared Parsons' face held a decided smirk, and Erica looked like a sleek feline, her eyes narrowed in amusement. Cathy felt awkward under their gaze and stumbled as she was walking away from the judging booth. She jammed the prize ribbon into her slacks' pocket. It was Jared Parsons' smirk that made her wish she had never won. Just who was he anyway, this man who had come to Swan Quarter and upset her like this? What did he do and why was everything so secret? The only thing she did know was that Erica was involved in the secret too. Cathy felt that if she knew what he did she could do a little sniping of her own, and at least she would feel better. It had often crossed her mind that Jared was involved in something illegal. That would explain his apparent wealth, at any rate.

Somehow, Cathy couldn't resolve herself to accepting the thought that Jared Parsons was linked with the underworld. There was an almost tangible aura of respectability about him; his clear gray eyes, his open smile. No, it was not to be considered, something in her rebelled, something she did not choose to put a name to. Perhaps Jared had inherited the wealth that supported his playboy life-style. She just wished she knew the answer. It would help erect her defenses against him.

But for now she had to get Bizzy from the kennel. He had proved his worth and came in second in the bird-dog class, it was time to take him home. The shaggy dog leaped for joy when Cathy came into view, his tail wagging furiously. "You're as fickle as that fiend out there. If he was here to open this door, you wouldn't pay any attention to me," Cathy said shortly, remembering Bizzy's unqualified loyalty to Jared. The moment the door of the cage was opened, Bismarc was off and running. No doubt to find his fickle friend, Cathy thought nastily. Now she would have to stomp the dusty festival grounds in search of the friendly dog.

Annoyed with herself and the world, Cathy settled down on a rustic bench and peeled the wrapper off a candy bar. Munching the crunchy sweet, she let her eyes rove the grounds for some sign of Bismarc. He was coming toward her at a dead run. She waited till he was near enough for her to reach out and grasp his collar. The dog backed off and barked, his front paws stamping the ground. He barked again and advanced a step and then withdrew. He barked louder and shook his head. He started off in the direction from which he had come and then turned to see if Cathy was following him. Again, he ran to her and backed off, barking wildly. "You want me to come with you, is that it?" Bismarc woofed loudly and this time ran off, Cathy on his heels.

Cathy's eyes took in the situation at the isolated river's edge behind the crab packaging building. Pieces of a homemade raft lay splintered on the shoreline and some distance out she could just make out flailing arms and almost hear a weak shout. She didn't hesitate. Quickly, she shed her wooden clogs and stripped off her slacks and hit the water at the same time Bismarc did. Her strokes were sure and powerful as she made her way to the swimmer in distress. Once she raised her head and saw the figure slide beneath the water. Frenzy drove her on as she prayed she wouldn't be too late. It must be a child, an inexperienced child, who had entered the contest with the homemade rafts. Probably a summer guest who wasn't too familiar with the river. The cry, when she heard it, was feeble and weak. It spurred her on. Her arms were getting tired, and there was a sharp pain in her shoulder. Bismarc barked behind her to show he was following her, his big paws daintily plunging into the water. "Hold on," Cathy called, "I'm coming. Tread water," she gasped as she herself began to tread and then struck out for the child who was almost within her grasp. "Chunky Williams!" she choked in dismay. Lord, she sighed, there was no way she was going to be able to tow him to shore. She was too tired and the boy was just too heavy, the complement of too many sweets and rich food. The most she could do was hold him upright and hope he hadn't taken in too much water. "Bizzy," she commanded, "go back and get Dad. Get somebody and *hurry!*" The Irish Setter remained in the water, his paws lapping at the wetness. He appeared uncertain, should he leave his mistress and the boy or should he obey the weak command? "Go!" Cathy ordered.

Cathy watched as Bismarc paddled through the water. "Go faster," she prayed, knowing full well the setter was doing his best.

"Th...thanks, Mi...Miss Bissette," Chunky said hoarsely. "I...I'm... so...cold."

"What happened?" Cathy asked, trying to keep the chubby boy's head above water as well as her own.

Chunky tried to grin and failed. "I... di... didn't use... rawhide when I bound the raft. I used mom's old clothesline, and it stretched when it got wet... everything just... fell apart... My dad is going to... sk... skin me alive."

"No, he won't," Cathy shivered. "He'll be so glad to see that you're okay, he'll just take you out to the woodshed for a little father-son talk."

"Gee... do... you... really think... so?"

"You have my word. Parents are like that. It was a dumb thing for you to do, coming out here alone on the river after the race," she gasped, struggling with his weight, treading water, trying to keep them both afloat. It would be useless to tell Chunky to float, he was too frightened, too tense.

"I hate coming in last," the boy grumbled. "Mom told me I didn't have a chance because all the other kids were skinnier and littler, but I wouldn't listen. Are we going to die, Miss Bissette?" he asked fearfully.

"Not if I can help it," Cathy replied through clenched teeth. "Look, Bizzy just got to shore. Any minute now Dad will be here with the boat and you can look forward to that talk in the woodshed. Don't give up now, Chunky," Cathy said, trying to shift the boy's weight to her left side. Her arms were numb and there didn't seem to be much feeling. Cathy recognized their peril, yet it was incomprehensible to her that she could die here in the river that had been her friend since she was a little girl. The sun was bright and hot and glistened on the calm water like spilled diamonds. People drowned in the dark, with wind-churned waters greedily reaching out for them, not in the glorious brightness of the Fourth of July. "Do you think you could float on your back, Chunky?"

"No. I ate too much pizza and ice cream before I came out here. I have terrible pains in my stomach." Cathy groaned as she searched the shoreline for some sign of help. Even from this distance she knew it was Jared Parsons who made the clean dive into the glistening river water. Bismarc stayed behind, barking wildly. Other people gathered, cheering the swimmer on with enthusiasm. "Hang on, Chunky, your savior is about to arrive," Cathy said in disgust. "Just you wait till I get my hands on that dog."

"What did you say, Miss Bissette? I can't hold up any longer," Chunky said, sliding through her weak hold on him as he clutched his mid-section.

Cathy slipped beneath the water and frantically searched for the boy. She had her arms beneath his armpits when she felt herself being shouldered out of the way. Gratefully, she surfaced and shook the water from her eyes.

Jared held the boy effortlessly as he stared deeply into Cathy's eyes. "While commendable, it was a foolish thing for you to do. Why didn't you get help before setting out here alone? How did you think one little slip of a girl was going to save this kid?" Not bothering to wait for a reply, he continued to scold. "Both of you could have drowned and that fool dog of yours is just about useless. Can you make it back to shore or should I call for someone to come and get you?''

"I can make it," Cathy said bitterly. "And you're wrong, Jared Parsons, my dog is not useless. If it wasn't for Bismarc, Chunky would be dead now. I did the best I could at the time. If it doesn't meet with your approval, it's just too...damn bad. And from now on, stay away from my dog!'' Cathy shot as she used every ounce of reserve she had to stroke out and head for shore.

Even towing in the heavy Chunky, Jared Parsons reached the river bank before she did. Men were clapping him on the back and women were oohing and aahing over him as he carefully laid Chunky on the ground. Some kind soul wrapped a blanket around Jared's shoulders as Bizzy licked at his toes in approval of his lifesaving venture. Tears streamed down Cathy's cheeks as she watched in amazement. They were ignoring her. The child she had kept aloft in the water, her dumb dog and her father were all crowded around the muscular Jared Parsons. No one offered her a blanket; no one asked if she was all right. "That does it!" she groaned. "That's it," she repeated to herself. "I'm going back to New York."

Cathy sniffed and hiccoughed all the way to the parking lot where she searched for the pick-up truck. Climbing behind the wheel, she drove home in a storm of tears.

Fresh from her second bath of the day, Cathy dressed again and dried her hair. Should she go back to the celebration or stay home? Dermott would be waiting for her, and the least she could do was tell him she was no longer interested in anything concerning the Fourth of July festival. Lord, she was tired. Surely, Dermott wouldn't expect her to enter the dance contest now. Who cares anyway? She poured herself a cup of strong, black coffee and immediately drank it as tears began to well in her eyes. The scalding coffee had the desired effect, and she squelched the tears. She was mad. She wanted to scream and kick, to lash out, hurt like she'd been hurt, the way she used to do when she was a child. She was grown up now and was expected to act like an adult. Ha! As far as she could tell, she had been the only one acting like a grown-up. Stupid, mysterious Jared Parsons, flighty, little girl in a woman's body, Erica, and Lucas in his second childhood. Who cares what they do; who cares what they think? Not me, she thought childishly. "I'm going back to New York as soon as I can get plane reservations." By now Jared would be the next thing to a national hero. Man of mystery saves little boy. Endears himself to all the residents of Swan Quarter. Mystery man steals dog's affection. Cathy grimaced. She admitted to herself that that was what hurt the most. Bizzy used to love her; they were inseparable, and for him to give his affection to that... that playboy was more than she could bear. This time the tears welled up and trickled down her cheeks. She sniffed and wiped at them with the back of her hand only to find more.

A shadow fell across the table and startled her. Cathy gulped and turned. "I looked for you but you were gone. I'm sorry if I seemed abrupt with you back there in the river, but I knew you needed something to make you angry. Angry enough to make you swim back on your own. You looked as done-in as the boy," Jared said softly. "For some strange reason, the mere sight of me seems to make you angry, and I thought...what I mean is..."

He was looking at her so strangely that she felt weak. She should be telling him off, giving him a piece of her mind, but she was just standing here, staring at him. She nodded, accepting his apology. She was certain it was an apology, the closest thing he would ever come to in taking the blame for anything. She accepted the snowy handkerchief and blew her nose. It smelled like Jared, and she held the linen cloth a second longer than necessary to her nose, savoring the manly scent of the man standing so close to her. When she did manage to get her wits together and speak, the calmness in her voice surprised her. "Where is my dog, Mr. Parsons?"

Jared Parsons smiled. "Believe it or not, he's sitting on the river bank, guarding your belongings." The old mocking ring was back in his voice. "You can hardly blame me if your dog likes me. Short of kicking him or

hitting him, what would you have me do? I
happen to like animals, dogs in particular,
and I guess Bismarc senses that." His eyes
wore an amused look as he waited for her to
speak. Cathy nodded and turned away.

"I'm going back to the celebration, can I
give you a lift?"

"No thank you," Cathy answered po-
litely.

"Then I suppose I'll see you later at the
dance contest. Erica and I are entering. She's
a superb dancer. I understand you and one
of the local boys are entering, at least that's
what Lucas said."

"And did my father tell you the local boy
also has two left feet?" Cathy asked quietly.

Jared Parsons gazed at Cathy, his head
tilted slightly to the side. "No, he didn't.
You don't seem to have a very high opinion
of your own worth, Miss Bissette. If you
don't, how do you expect other people to
measure you?"

"It's not the measuring that I mind,"
Cathy snapped, "it's the comparisons I object to." Jared Parsons understood perfectly, just as she had intended. He closed

the door behind him, and to Cathy it was the most terminal sound she had ever heard.

Cathy waited silently next to Dermott McIntyre in the makeshift ballroom that was to be used for the disco contest. She knew Erica was nearby by the heady scent which wafted about her. Dermott's myopic gaze was all the proof she needed. She felt tacky next to the svelte, long-limbed woman who was smiling at her. "I never won a cup in my life. Jared says he's confident we'll win. We've danced at all 'the' clubs in New York City on more than one occasion. Have you, Miss Bissette?"

"No," Cathy replied shortly. "I... I wish you luck."

"Luck has nothing to do with it. Jared and I have perfected our routine over the past months. We dance very well, and from what I've seen of the entrants," she said, looking around disdainfully, "I see no competition. You aren't entering, are you?" It wasn't so much a question but a statement of fact.

"I wouldn't think of it," Cathy said quietly, nudging Dermott to remain quiet. If his life depended on it, he wouldn't have been able to speak, he was so busy eyeing the mid-thigh slit on the satin skirt and the matching spike heels that Erica wore to perfection. "Well, here comes Jared," Erica bubbled. Cathy couldn't bear the thought of dancing now.

"But I thought you wanted to enter this contest," Dermott complained. "I polished my shoes for nothing. Why, just tell me why?"

"Because we aren't good enough, and I have no desire to see you make a fool of yourself. We wouldn't have a chance against them," Cathy said, nodding in Jared Parsons' direction. Her eyes took in the white silk shirt, open almost to his waist, with his bronze chest showing and the made-for-his-hips black pants. He was the focal point of every woman's eye and the envy of every man. It was evident in the way the young men hugged their young ladies to their sides. Dermott was not immune to Jared's threatening charms. Protectively, he put his arm around her waist. "That guy's a rover," he said curtly, never taking his eyes off Erica.

Cathy bristled. "If he's a rover, what does that make Erica?"

Dermott blushed.

"Oh, really?" Cathy asked happily, taking Dermott's flush of color for an answer.

"You bet, guys like that smoothie love 'em and leave 'em, I know their type. I'm a man," he said proudly.

Cathy wanted to tell Dermott next to a man like Jared Parsons he was a mere boy, but she held her tongue. Dermott was nice, perhaps he was too nice for her. He might have two left feet, but he had other sterling qualities which would endear him to some other young woman.

Suddenly, Dermott didn't seem to mind that they weren't going to enter the contest. He was affable, his eyes glued to the voluptuous figure of Erica who was holding out her hand for her card number. Jared, as always, looked loose, ready for anything, and Cathy knew the striking pair would win the contest hands down.

"Who decorated the hall, and where did that band come from?" Dermott asked.

Cathy looked around the makeshift ball-room and had to admire the artistic decor. The multi-colored flashing lights and the ear-splitting warm-up music made for a gala night with all the proceeds going to the local orphanage. "Pat Laird and John Cuomo are responsible, at least that's what Dad told me. Al Anderson rigged up the lights. Billy Jensen's band has played all over the South, so I expect we're going to have a sell-out. They're good, aren't they?" Cathy shouted to be heard over the din.

"Yeah, great," Dermott replied, his eye on Erica's long leg, flashing through the slit in her skin-tight skirt.

If I'm lucky, she'll get a cramp, Cathy thought nastily and immediately was sorry for wishing ill on the beautiful girl. I'm just jealous, she admitted to herself.

"What number are you and Dermott?" Lucas Bissette asked, coming up behind Cathy and laying his hand on her shoulder.

"We're not entering," Cathy said quietly. Lucas stepped in front of Cathy and stared down into her eyes.

"Can't handle it, eh, Cat?"

A sharp retort rose to Cathy's lips. Good heaven, what was happening to her when she couldn't handle her father's jibes? Cathy swallowed hard and said very softly, "That's exactly right, Dad, I can't handle it. And this is as good a time as any to tell you I'll be leaving the middle of the week. Make whatever you want out of that."

Lucas Bissette again patted Cathy fondly on the shoulder, then hugged her. "Whatever you do is okay with me, Cat, you know that." Cathy's eyes widened at his paternal tone. Then Lucas put the sting back in. "You're the one who has to live with yourself," he muttered as he walked away.

"What did your dad say?" Dermott asked as he shifted from one foot to the other.

"He said I was a Polish princess and I deserved a Polish prince, and since there isn't a prince available, he understood why I wasn't entering the contest," Cathy grimaced.

"Izat right?" Dermott grinned, watching the first contestants take to the floor.

Cathy watched the first four contestants with clinical objectivity. They were good, but they lacked the skills she knew she was going to see when Erica and Jared took to the floor. She felt defenseless, vulnerable as she watched the fifth couple make their way to the middle of the floor. Her eyes traveled the circle of people who were breathlessly watching the dancers. At this point she needed some paternal protection. Dermott was oblivious to her departure as she worked her way through the milling circle of people to stand next to her father. He looked at her and smiled. Cathy sighed, he understood.

"Cat, I'm taking Erica into town after the contest. I just happened to mention to her that the Lobster Pit was owned by a friend and..."

"Dad, you don't have to explain to me what you do. In turn I expect the same courtesy from you."

"I just wanted you to know where I would be in..."

"In case I needed you. And that also means Mr. Parsons is free and available." The two twirling contestants ended their number with their arms outstretched to applause. Cathy joined in, her mind whirling with excitement. Dad was taking Erica to the Lobster Pit. Jared Parsons would drive her home if her father had anything to say about it. Surely, Lucas wouldn't have the nerve to take the ravishing Erica to the Pit in the pickup which meant he would take the Mark IV. Girls like Erica didn't ride in trucks. Girls like Cathy Bissette who won cooking contests rode in pick-ups.

Cathy clenched her fists tightly to her side as Erica led Jared to the middle of the dance floor. It was quiet, more quiet than when the other contestants had made their way to the center of the floor, possibly because most of the people in the room knew the dancers. Erica and Jared were strangers, New York strangers, sophisticated people with money. Cathy looked around and was stunned at the looks on the faces of the crowd. The women, old and young alike, wore admiring looks, and the men were openly leering at Erica who was smiling widely. No one had that many teeth, Cathy grimaced. Then her eyes widened when she glanced at Jared who wore a mocking smile and was staring directly at her. Darn it, he had seen the grimace and probably thought she was jealous, which she was, she admitted honestly to herself. She startled herself when she mouthed silently, good luck. Jared lost the mocking smile and stared at her as if she had said something obscene. Then she further amazed herself by waving and smiling at the couple.

"Good girl, Cat, I knew you could handle it," Lucas grinned.

"You know something, Dad, you might just be right. The music is starting. Here's your chance to see what they do back in the Big Apple."

They were fluid, their movements perfectly tuned to one another as they twirled and moved to the wild beat of the music. There was no envy in Cathy now, only appreciation of the dancers and their movements. The dance over, Cathy clapped wildly with the crowd. It was obvious that they won and the Master of Ceremonies was making his way to the middle of the floor to present the gold cup to Erica, who accepted it graciously. Jared was smiling and accepting the congratulations of the young crowd. He smiled down at a little gray-haired lady and then unexpectedly kissed her on the cheek. The woman brought a dry, wrinkled hand to her cheek in awe and then smiled happily.

Unreasonable rage coursed through Cathy. Steals dogs, kisses me whenever he feels like it, bamboozles my father, and endears himself to old ladies. "He'd make an excellent politician. I bet he even kisses babies," she said tartly to her father.

"There's nothing wrong with kissing babies. I've kissed a few in my day," Lucas grinned.

"I'm hungry, Dad, I think I'll get myself a hot dog or something. I don't see Dermott around anywhere, so if you see him, tell him where I am."

"Will do. Time to claim my prize. Do you want me to bring you some lobster back from the Pit?"

"No thanks, a hot dog will be fine. I guess I won't see you till morning. Have a good time, Dad," Cathy said, walking into the crowd.

Her hot dog finished, there was no sign of Dermott. Hopefully, he found something to occupy himself and he had forgotten her. She picked at her French fries and let her eyes rove the crowd. There was no sign of Jared Parsons. She felt annoyed. She would give him another few minutes, and if he didn't show up, she would go on home and let him find his way back to his boat on his own. If she went home now, she would miss the fireworks. She smiled secretly and then laughed. If Jared did show up, he was quite capable of making his own fireworks, only it would be Cathy Bissette who exploded, not the suave, debonair Jared Parsons. If, and it looked right now like a mighty big if, he showed up and drove her home, she was going to make up her mind not to act like a child. Behaving like a child was what made her lose Marc back in New York. She would act like the enlightened New Yorker her father kept telling her she was.

Fifteen minutes went by and then another fifteen and still no Jared. The couple working in the hot dog stand were beginning to stare at her. Time to move on. Time to go home. Alone. What had she expected really? That Jared was going to fall all over her and declare undying love.

Yep, Cathy thought. And right now I'd even settle for a lie. Tears gathered in her eyes, and she was glad it was dark as she made her way to the pick-up truck and found Bizzy sitting in the back of the payloader. She slid behind the wheel and the tears brimmed over and slid down her cheeks. Childishly, she wiped at them with the back of her hand. A sob caught in her throat. She stifled it and sniffed, needing to blow her nose. The offer of the snowy piece of linen, when it was offered, made her gasp.

"Your father asked me to drive you home, and I've been combing this infernal fair ground for the past hour. The least you could do is stay put in one spot," Jared said coolly as he motioned for her to slide over so he could take the wheel.

Cathy stared at him. Duty. He was only taking her home because her father asked him to, and he needed a ride to get back to his boat. Thank heaven he couldn't read her expression. "Don't do me any favors," she said through clenched teeth just as the first Roman candle exploded into a kaleidoscope of color and sound.

Jared Parsons ignored the fireworks and stuck his head out the window to back up the pick-up truck. When he faced the road again, the same wry smile played around the corners of his mouth. "Fireworks always remind me of a woman's emotions. Up and down, explosive and then . . . fizzle."

"You're insufferable. Still, if anyone should know about women, I suppose a man like you is the one to be an expert," Cathy said huffily, aware of the effect his nearness was having on her.

Jared's voice was harsh and somehow tender when he spoke. "What's that supposed to mean?"

"It means whatever you want it to mean," Cathy retorted, glad that she had gotten a rise out of the man. Quietly, she drew in her breath, marvelling at the sensuous expertise with which he was handling the old pick-up. She felt like she was in the Mark IV and they were both in evening clothes.

"I get the impression you don't like me very much. Why is that, Miss Bissette?"

Cathy felt confused. Deny it or ignore the question. She opted for truth. "I don't know if I like or dislike you. All I know is I feel very uncomfortable around you. I don't like the feeling. If that means I don't like you, then I'm sorry."

Jared laughed and pulled the truck over to the side of the road.

The nightsong of the birds was music to Cathy's ears, and the dark night was a velvet cocoon where she rested in anticipation of her own Roman candle showering the two of them with emotion. Trembling, she inched away from his outstretched arms. How could a man, any man, have this effect on her? She wanted the feel of his arms around her as much as she wanted to draw another breath. What she didn't want was for Jared Parsons to know how she felt. Trembling women were something he was no doubt used to, and she didn't want to be just another one of his entourage of shaking, quaking, giddy women who fell all over themselves and then fell apart when he left them for someone new. But before she realized it she was giving herself up to the moment.

Chapter Seven

Cathy heard the low sound deep in his chest as he reached across the seat for her. His fingers tightened on her shoulders, drawing her to him. She felt his warm breath in her hair, felt his lips against her ear and in the soft hollow beneath it. The crush of his mouth against her lips evoked a taunting fire that flared and raced through her veins. She was helpless, powerless against him. She fleetingly thought of all the vows she had made to repel him, to be safe from his lure, and consumed by the fire within, they went up in billows of smoke. All she knew, all she was aware of, was that this was Jared and she, Cathy, was in his arms, tasting his lips upon her own and reveling in the delights of awakened passion that he stirred within her.

Her arms wound around his neck, holding him, pressing her own mouth against his in an answering kiss. Her lips parted, her fingers wound in the dark, silky hair at the nape of his neck. She could feel the strength of him in his embrace, feel his breath against her cheek, feel her power as a woman who was wanted and desirable.

His hands caressed her throat, his fingers trailed down the length of the graceful column, and she could feel her pulses beating against his touch.

The tailored, blue checked blouse she wore was opened to the cleavage between her breasts, and when his hand slid inside and grazed her skin, it sent off little charges of electricity which sparked and caused her to gasp for breath. Masterfully, he slowly undid her top button. His hand caressed her skin, molding itself to the curves of her body, ardently searching for its fullness in the cup of his palm.

Cathy's breath quickened with yearning as his touch ignited a flame on her already heated skin. She was losing herself, aware only of him, the scent of him, the strength of him, wanting only to know him. His effect on her was more heady than French wine and her senses reeled and whirled, making it impossible for her to think, to make any protest. She was a woman and she wanted, needed.

Jared released her mouth at last, his lips leaving hers slowly, reluctantly. He began a searching, tender exploration of the curve of her throat, his lips finding her pulse and resting there, seeming to draw the vitality from her. Her mouth pouted with passion and a longing climbed the length of her spine as his gentle caresses became deeper, more sensuous. He seemed to know instinctively where her vulnerabilities slept—in the hollow of her throat, in the valley between her breasts.

She found herself straining toward him, offering herself to him, welcoming him with her embrace. She heard a soft sound of pleasure and suddenly realized it was the sound of her own voice, coming from somewhere deep within her, from a hidden part of her that she had never explored.

There was an ache deep within her, and it was echoed in her response. Her lips sought his, finding and searching. Her fingers grazed his chest, sliding over the muscular expanse of it and stopping to wander through the soft furring she found there.

She heard her name on his lips, and the husky sound of it made her weak with longing. The moment became her eternity as she lost herself in her need for Jared.

His hands took possession of her, feathering against her soft skin. His kiss was a drug, his arms a prison, the sound of her name on his lips was food for her passion. There was only the here and now, only herself and Jared lived in the world, and he was a man and she a woman. Nothing, no one, mattered except that she was here in his arms and he was making love to her, loving her.

Her voice, when she heard it, was husky and passion filled. It was the only sound that broke the quiet of the night. "Jared," she spoke his name like a cry, a sound born of her soul and birthed on her lips. She offered herself to him, pressing against the touch of his hand, moving against him, lost in her need for him.

Imperceptibly, she was aware that his lips gave no answering response. That his hands had become still and that he was drawing away from her. What had she done? What had she said? Why had he released her from his embrace and was now looking through the windshield out into the darkness.

"Jared?"

"Button your blouse, Cathy." His voice was hard, stern, void of the emotions she could have sworn he had been feeling only a moment ago.

Ignoring his orders, only aware that right now, this moment, she needed to hear from his own lips the reason for his sudden coldness. She asked, "Why?" Even she could hear the choked sob behind her question; she could feel her eyes burning with tears.

He turned to look at her, his eyes burning her flesh as they glanced over her, taking in her open blouse that revealed much of her breasts. His eyes were cold and flinty, and even in the darkness she could see the flash of his white teeth as he smiled wryly. "Someone told me, Miss Bissette, quite confidentially, of course, that you were saving yourself for marriage."

He was laughing at her, mocking her and all her newly found tender emotions. He had made a fool of her. No, that was wrong. She had made a fool of herself, throwing herself at him, offering herself to him, wanting him as a woman wanted a man. She had been ready to satisfy their passions and now he was laughing at her. And to further her own humiliation, she had asked him why. The question itself had been tantamount to begging, pleading, imploring him to take her for his own.

With shaking fingers she redid the buttons on her blouse. "Forget I asked that question. I really don't care to hear the answer. I think you should know that you're the most insufferable man I've ever met. You are selfish and self-serving and you hurt people, Jared Parsons," Cathy hissed. "And you've got the hungriest eyes of any man I've ever met. Get out of my truck!'' With a force that was surprising, she tried to shove him over to the side of the seat and push him out the door.

"Wait a minute," Jared laughed. "It's the girl who's supposed to walk home. You don't understand. I wasn't making fun of you. Not at all. I was only trying to respect you..." He was at a loss for words.

"Go ahead! Say it!" Cathy spit angrily. "Say what you're thinking. Go ahead, say 'your virginity.'" Doubling her hand into a fist, she lashed out, hitting him squarely in the eye. "That's for making fun of me, and this," she added, socking him again on the chin, "is for stealing my dog's affections. I hate you, Jared Parsons! I hate you! And if you ever come near me again...I...I'll..."

Her emotions were choking off all thought. Gathering the shreds of her dignity, Cathy swung open the truck door and jumped out and ran away down the road. She ran, away from Jared Parsons, as fast as her legs could carry her. Bizzy jumped down from the back and raced after her, his bark breaking the stillness of the night.

Cathy moped around the kitchen, the Irish Setter on her heels. It had been three days since she last saw Jared Parsons. Angrily, she kicked out at the stove with her sandaled foot and immediately let out a howl of pain. He was out there, sequestered with the delectable Erica, doing only God knows what. It was her own fault; she had said she never wanted to see him again. The morning after their last encounter the pick-up truck had been parked in the driveway, the only reminder that she had been in it with Jared Parsons. She felt her father knew something, but there was no way she was going to ask him even one word about Mr. Parsons.

The telephoned shrilled, and Cathy debated a moment before picking it up. It might be Jared. "Hello," she said cautiously. "Mr. Denuvue, what's wrong, why are you calling me here?" she asked fearfully. She listened a moment. "Of course I do. Why me? Tomorrow! Yes, yes, I can be there. Thank you, Mr. Denuvue, for giving me the opportunity. I'll do my best." Cathy stared at the phone a minute before replacing the receiver back in its cradle. "Bizzy, did you hear that?" she cried excitedly. "That was Mr. Denuvue, the president of the publishing house I work for, and he just told me I'm going to be Teak Helm's new editor. Mrs. English decided to go to California to live with her daughter who is expecting her first child. She gave up Teak Helm for a baby. I have to be in New York in the morning, which means I have to leave tonight. But, if I leave now, I'll never see Jared again. I was so excited when Mr. Denuvue called, I almost forgot about Jared. What am I going to do?" She reached for the telephone only to withdraw her hand. Three days and three nights on the boat with Erica. Why should he care if she went back to New York? She said she never wanted to see him again. How could he believe such a blatant lie? She was the one who said it, and she knew it was a lie. He was supposed to be an expert where women were concerned. Didn't he know a lie when he heard one? Of course not, she said disgustedly to the setter. He was the one who told the lies. All men lie.

It was a once in a lifetime offer; she couldn't turn it down, not even for a man like Jared Parsons. She would be a fool if she didn't go back to New York and take the job offer. In just a few days Jared's boat would be repaired, and he would sail off and never give her a second thought. So, why was she standing here even thinking of not accepting the offer? "And," she said to the sleeping dog, "I'll be making a lot more money, and I won't have to scrimp and save. Maybe I could get a bigger apartment that will take dogs and then you can come and live with me. Wouldn't that be great?" Bismarc ignored her as she rambled on, her voice breaking each time she mentioned Jared's name. "I'm going to accept the offer," she said firmly to the dog. "First, I'll pack and then we'll take the skiff out for one last ride, after that it's goodbye Swan Quarter till Christmas."

Inside of an hour she had her bags packed and her room straightened up. Quickly, she called the airline and made a plane reservation. It was now definite. She was accepting the offer and returning to New York.

Cathy packed a meager lunch for herself along with a fresh double bag of Oreo cookies for Bismarc. At the last minute she wrote her father a note and left it on the table. She didn't want him to think she was leaving in anger or in a pique over something or other; namely, Jared Parsons. He would understand about the job offer and be the first one to tell her to accept. Plus she knew Lucas would want to drive her to the airport.

The weather was typical for July in North Carolina. The sun beat down mercilessly and the humidity was high. Bizzy sat in the bow of the outboard and allowed the breeze to stroke his russet coat. Out on the river, alone with only Bizzy, Cathy regretted her decision to leave Swan Quarter for the sultry New York summer. This was home, where she belonged, with the sky and sun and the river, not in the concrete jungle with the smog created by the taxis and buses and the hectic coming and going of the subways. Here was God's country and she loved it.

The motor created a wide wake behind her, and once or twice she heard the engine cough in protest. Dad had been promising to give it an overhaul, but apparently he had never gotten around to it. And now, at the height of the shrimping and crabbing season, he had committed himself to repair Jared Parsons' yacht. "That leaves you and me out in the cold," she said, as she patted the motor housing, "just don't give up on me now." As though hearing her words, the engine returned to full power, and she made a heading for the beach on the point.

When she approached shore, she cut off the engine, drifting into the sandy beach until the keel scraped bottom. Quickly, from long years of practice, she climbed over the side into knee-high water and carried the Danforth anchor ashore, burying it securely into the sand. "C'mon, Bizzy," she encouraged as she lifted her lunch and an old blanket to take ashore. "This is our last day here till winter, let's enjoy it."

The afternoon was an idyll spent in the sun, playing with her dog and enjoying the cool, refreshing waters of the Pamlico River. Drying off from her last swim, she glanced at her watch. Plenty of time to get home and bathe and do her hair before leaving for the airport. She hoped Lucas was home and that she wouldn't have to scout him down. She knew her father would be disappointed that she was leaving so suddenly, but he would understand. Lucas was a business man, and he knew you had to get while the getting was good. This was too great an opportunity to pass by.

Bizzy took his place in the bow while she set the engine to start and whipped the cord, expecting to hear it roar to life. Nothing. Dead. Again she tried, again nothing.

Exasperated, she lifted back the motor housing and fiddled with the spark plug. Again she tried. Nothing. She did all the things she thought she was supposed to do, even going so far as checking the gas tank, knowing full well that Lucas never left a boat on empty. Still nothing.

She was stranded, marooned. Not on an island, but on a slim strip of beach that was backed by thick woods and stubborn undergrowth. She looked back in the direction of the tall trees and moaned. This was a place that was only accessible by boat. If she had to make it to the road, she would find herself faced with three or four miles of forest primeval.

Bizzy whined as though sensing her dilemma. "Might as well come ashore, Biz. It doesn't look as though we're going anywhere. Not for a while, at least."

The sun had swung into the western sky and was beginning to dip to the horizon. She kept a careful eye peeled for a passing boat and even had her beach towel ready to flag it down. But boat traffic at this end of the Pamlico was a sparse and almost nonexistent thing on a weekday. With a groan, Cathy lowered herself to the sand and waited.

She looked at her watch for what she thought was the hundredth time and winced. If she wasn't found soon, she would miss the plane. Where was her father? Didn't he get her note? Surely, he would have read it by now and realized the time. Fathers were supposed to worry about their children. He knew where she always went with the skiff to picnic and read and swim. Maybe he didn't want her going back to New York, and he was deliberately making himself unavail-

able. He could have come in and read the
note and decided to pretend he hadn't come
home in time to take her to the airport.

No, that was silly. That wasn't like Dad at
all. Closer to the truth was that he was still
working on Jared's yacht and hadn't even
bothered to come home at all.

Out in the distance was a small object, and
she immediately recognized that it was a
boat long before she could hear the engine.
Jumping to her feet, she stood on the point's
headland and began to wave her beach towel
furiously. "Bark, Bizzy! Maybe they'll hear
you!" She knew it was improbable, but Bismarc's shiny red coat might catch their attention as he raced up and down the beach.

It seemed to take an eternity for the craft
to come within distance, and when it did,
Cathy's heart sank. Jared's runabout!

Shifting her thoughts into neutral, she
went back to the skiff and readied its lines
for towing.

The minute she heard his voice she felt
sick to her stomach. She had thought she
could push down her emotions at him finding her and the memory of the night of the

July fourth celebration. Of all the people in the world, why did it have to be Jared Parsons who found her? She would have rather taken her chances with a barracuda.

Jared's face was cold and aloof as he stared at her and smiled. "Your father is working on my engine and, rather than have him stop, I told him I would look for you. Don't you ever think before you jump on your impulses? Lucas said you knew the skiff wasn't ready for water, so why did you take it out? Did you want me to come looking for you?"

Cathy's own voice matched his coolness. She was glad his presence hadn't started her limbs shaking as they usually did. Her blue eyes were steady and her mouth was a grim, tight line. "The reason my skiff isn't ready is because my dad has spent all his time working on your yacht. And, no, I didn't expect or want you to come rescue me. In another few hours you won't have to worry about me. I'm taking the evening plane to New York. In short, Mr. Parsons, you'll have no need to wet nurse me ever again." Cathy could see her words and tone surprised him by the way his eyes narrowed. As if she cared what he thought.

The ride back to Lucas Bissette's pier was uneventful. Jared kept his back to her, his hands clenched on the wheel. As soon as the boat slid next to the pier, Cathy was up and off with no help from the man at the wheel. Bismarc leaped to the pier and stood barking loudly at both man and girl. "Thank you for bringing me home," Cathy said formally. "I'm sorry for any inconvenience I may have caused you. I know what a busy man you must be," she said in a syrupy sweet voice. Jared stared at her, a frown on his face. He made no comment. He was making her uncomfortable again. After today, she wouldn't have to worry about feeling like that again. Even to her ears her formal, quiet goodbye sounded final. Turning on her heel, she walked the length of the pier, Bismarc trotting alongside. Tears blurred her vision, but the dog at her side guided her expertly to the shore.

By midnight she would be back in her little studio apartment about to embark on a new phase of life and this brief interlude would be nothing but a memory. "Why," she said heartbreakingly to the dog, "couldn't it be more than a memory?" Because it wasn't meant to be, she thought, squaring her shoulders.

Chapter Eight

Swan Quarter and Jared Parsons behind her, Cathy rolled the Teak Helm galleys into a tight bundle and with a deep breath walked into Walter Denuvue's office. If she was going to be Helm's new editor, then Walter had to be told now that she wouldn't be responsible for the sorry mess she held in her hands.

The social amenities and the congratulations over with, Cathy held the tightly rolled bundle in front of her, offering them to Walter Denuvue. "It's a mess, I can't take the responsibility for the manuscript. Have you read it?'' she asked bluntly.

''I'm sorry to say, no. However, before Margaret English left she brought me up to date on it. I did glance over it,'' Mr. Denuvue said defensively. ''You see, Cathy, Margaret had no desire to anger Mr. Helm. She tried to get him to do revisions and he refused. As a matter of fact, he claimed it was one of his best novels and went so far as to tell us if we changed one word he would change publishers. As long as we're going to be honest, we might as well be brutally honest. This house stays in business because of Teak's two novels a year. Without him we'd never get out of the red. If he threatens to pull out, then we have to go along with what he wants. We're a small publishing house and we need him.''

''If he's so independent and so arrogant, why does he need an editor? What can I do except correct his grammar; and if what you say is true, I can't even do that. I thought you brought me back here to be his editor in every sense of the word, not just someone at whom he can take pot shots.''

Walter Denuvue shook his shaggy white head. "We can't risk alienating him; his new novel is due the first of next month. Teak Helm wants an editor and you're it. You're right about one thing, he takes pot shots from time to time, and I'm not proud of the fact that I've allowed Margaret to go home in tears on more than one occasion. I hate it, but my hands are tied. There are people I have to answer to, stockholders among them."

"When is Mr. Helm due to come to the office?" Cathy asked quietly.

Walter Denuvue sighed. "Teak doesn't come to the office. He sends his manuscripts by messenger. I've personally never met him nor has anyone on my staff. You know, he doesn't have an agent. Actually, when it comes right down to it, he's a man of mystery, and none of us has ever been able to figure out why he's so keen on privacy and secrecy."

"Where do you mail his money?" Cathy demanded, not believing what she was hearing.

"We mail it directly to his bank."

"And there's nothing we can do except accept his demands and publish whatever he sends in, in the condition it arrives?"

"That's about the size of it, Cathy. I know I didn't do you any favors by giving you this job. You'll be working on other things, so the best I can tell you is not to let it get you down."

Cathy wasn't finished. "Walter, if you want to get in touch with him, how do you go about it?"

"We don't. That was one of the conditions. Actually, it's weird in a way. He always seems to know when we need to talk to him and he calls. That, you see, is one of the conditions of his contracts. He always delivers right on schedule, never been a day late in the eleven years we've done business. Look, Cathy, I don't want you trying to stir anything up by trying to get in touch with the bank. Margaret English tried that one time and within three hours Teak Helm was on the phone blasting us and threatening to go to another publisher. He's a regular demon when it comes to privacy."

Cathy felt deflated. "I understand everything you've just told me. However, I want to ask you something. Will you give me your permission to do a revision letter with suggestions and mail it out to the bank? I'll do it on my own time, and I'll be most careful how I word it. If we lose just this one manuscript, hopefully, Mr. Helm will get the message and not make the same mistakes on the forthcoming novel. It's worth a chance, Walter. How long do you think the readers will continue to buy his books if they aren't up to the standards of his others? Two books, tops, and we both know it."

Walter Denuvue thought a moment. He nodded. "It's worth a try. Cathy, be very careful how you make the suggestions." The old man looked winsome for a second, "Just how bad is it?"

"Bad," Cathy said succinctly. "I can't believe that as publisher of this house you haven't read it."

Walter Denuvue shrugged. "I'm into motorcycles and fast cars. If you want the truth," he said sheepishly, "I was never able to get past the first page of any of his books. That's not for publication,'' he said sternly.

Cathy grinned, her mind already composing her cover letter to one Teak Helm, author of seafaring adventures.

One day raced into another as Cathy pored industriously over the Teak Helm galleys. She worked in the office and then she went home to cook herself a sketchy dinner and then worked again until the wee hours of the morning. By the end of the third week back in New York she had her letter finished and, along with her suggested revisions, ready for mailing. How was the illustrious Teak Helm going to treat the contents of the manila envelope? She wrote the word, *urgent,* in capital letters on the envelope and then added stamps.

She was tired, exhausted really, from all the hard work she had been doing. She missed her father, Bismarc and Swan Quarter. Christmas seemed forever away. And Jared Parsons, where was he and what was he doing? As always, when she thought of Jared Parsons, she felt a hollow well grow in her stomach and her breathing would quicken. She had been grateful for the hard work she was doing on the galleys and was even more grateful when she climbed into bed, her eyes closing with just the thought of sleep. She felt she had weathered the emotional storm of parting from her memory of Jared Parsons by diving full force into work. If that was true, she asked herself, why was she sitting here thinking of him now?

When thoughts of Jared Parsons invaded her mind, as they had in the past weeks, Cathy forced herself to think of other things or to do something physical. She reached for a sweater and picked up the envelope. She would walk the six blocks to the nearest mail box and drop the envelope in the bright blue box. She would jog home and accomplish two things at once.

The moment the envelope slid into the mail box Cathy felt as if a weight had been lifted from her slim shoulders. How was the secretive Teak Helm going to respond to her letter and suggested revisions? Probably demand that Walter Denuvue fire her, that's how, she told herself.

As she jogged along, Cathy wished Bismarc was with her and then changed her mind. The big dog, used to roaming the river edge, would not like all the concrete and steel of New York. Maybe I should get a cat or something, she mused, as she skidded to a stop in front of her apartment building. Someday, she muttered, as she fit the key in the lock. Now, she was going to take a nice hot bath and make herself a cup of black rum tea and then go to sleep. She deserved a good eight hours of rest.

Cathy did sleep, fitfully, her dreams invaded by a tall, muscular man with gray eyes and a wry smile playing around his mouth as he chased her along the river bank in Swan Quarter. She woke, exhausted and hostile to her new day. A hot shower and a quick cup of strong black coffee made her, if not fit, willing to start the day.

Each time the phone rang she flinched. By the end of the day her tired sighs were the speculation of everyone in the office. She almost collapsed when the work day ended and there had been no word. When Margaret English had the audacity to get in touch with the bank officer, she had heard within three hours. Was it good or bad that she hadn't heard?

The days crawled by on tortoise legs. It had been almost a month to the day since she had mailed the manila envelope. In just two days Teak Helm's new manuscript was due. Would it arrive on time? What would it be like?

Cathy sat at her desk, her pencil poised over a manuscript she was supposed to be editing. She squinted at the printed words that held no meaning, wondering why in the world she was sitting there doing nothing; why she couldn't concentrate. She should be able to put it all behind her and concentrate on the day's work. She was too tired, too angry with her circumstances to realize what she was doing, she told herself. She had a job; she hadn't been fired by Walter Denuvue and that should count for something. Let Teak Helm and Jared Parsons do whatever they wanted. She had to pick up her life if it wasn't too late.

She had turned down all her friends' friendly invitations, been short with them on the phone, pleading one excuse after another until, finally, they stopped calling. She was alone and she didn't like the feeling. She needed a friend, a confidant. But, there was no one. Not even Bismarc was around to hear her sorry laments. She would spend another lonely night at home in the tiny apartment after a quick dinner of soup and a few crackers. One of these days, she told herself, she was going to cook herself a real dinner and put some of the flesh back on her bones. And what, she questioned, could be done about the dark circles around her eyes and her hollow cheeks? Makeup was wonderful, but it could camouflage just so much.

Cathy looked at the circlet of gold on her wrist and then at the big clock with the Roman numerals on the wall. Fifteen more minutes and she could go home. She looked around the office and noticed that no one appeared to be doing any work. She reached for her purse in her desk drawer and made her way to the ladies' room to repair the ravages of the day. She thought she heard her phone ring but decided she was mistaken.

No one ever called her at this time of day so there was no reason for concern.

Deftly, she applied fresh eye shadow and then applied a beige cream to the circles beneath her eyes. A quick brush with the rouge pot and a dap of lipstick completed the job. Perfume? Why not? Even bus drivers need a little diversion after smelling exhaust fumes all day. She patted a few drops of VanCleef and Arpell's *First* behind her ears and at the hollow of her throat. She washed her hands, dried them and took another look in the bright mirror, wishing they would use less wattage. She would mention that to Walter tomorrow. A rosy forty watt bulb would be just perfect.

Cathy looked around the office and wasn't surprised to see that aside from one of the mail boys the office was empty. A bright pink message slip caught her eye on her desk. She peered at the scrawl and almost fainted. "Teak Helm called. He will call tomorrow morning. He sounded angry."

"Billy, who took this message, do you know?" Cathy shouted to the mail boy.

"I did, Miss Bissette. Why, did I do something wrong?" the boy asked anxiously.

"No, no, of course not. How do you know that Mr. Helm was angry?" she asked past the lump in her throat.

"Because he sounded just like my dad when my mother bangs up the car or when I let the car run out of gas," Billy said shortly. "He said he would call you back in the morning. I told him you were in the ladies' room and that you would be right out, but he said he couldn't hold on the wire."

"It's okay, Billy. Go on home. I'll see you tomorrow, and thanks for taking my message."

That night sleep was out of the question. Cathy paced the tiny apartment, her emotions in a turmoil. She hadn't felt this way since she left Jared Parsons in Swan Quarter. Was she falling apart? What was Teak Helm going to say to her? Would it end up being his way? Was she supposed to act like Margaret English when he called and yes the man to death? Did she dare defend her suggestions for revisions?

Cathy rubbed at her throbbing temples, willing the ache to leave her. Everything seemed to be going wrong with her. She knew she was run down and not sleeping right. Vitamins just went so far. She hadn't had a good night's sleep since leaving Swan Quarter. And now there wasn't going to be any sleep at all.

Curling up on the chocolate sofa, she longed for Bismarc and her father. Someone to talk to, to confide in. Someone with objectivity. Her eyes went to the sunburst clock over the bookcase—11:20. Seven more hours before she could shower and leave for work. She felt marked, like the eye of the devil was upon her. The worst thing that could happen would be that Teak Helm would ask for a new editor and have her fired. The best thing that could happen would be that Teak Helm would say he agreed with her suggestions and rewrite his book. Or, she thought morosely, he would have second thoughts and not call her at all and just let things lay.

Cathy reached for a note pad and pencil that lay next to the phone. She swiftly calculated her finances and decided that she could say on in the small apartment for approximately six months if she was fired. With her small savings account and her unemployment compensation, she might be able to stretch it to eight months. But would the unemployment office pay her if she was fired? If they didn't, she would only last in the apartment three months and that was stretching it a bit. If she sold her furniture piece by piece, she might be able to extend it a bit longer. Why was she torturing herself like this?

The phone shrilled, startling her. Who would be calling her at 11:45? All her friends had deserted her. Who could it be? In her befuddled state it didn't occur to her to pick up the phone. She sat staring at the squat black instrument in something akin to horror. She just knew that somehow Teak Helm had found out where she lived and gotten her number from the information operator. From everything she heard about the man he wouldn't think anything of calling someone at midnight to go through a tirade. Just like that insufferable Jared Parsons. No consid-

eration for anyone else's feelings. "Well, I'm
not going to answer it. I have an office and I
do business in it, not at home, at midnight," she said loudly and clearly.

The shrilling phone followed her into the
kitchen and lasted all the while she made
herself a cup of tea. It continued to shriek at
her as she cut herself a chunk of Monterey
Jack cheese, and it was still shrieking as she
carried the plate full with crackers into the
living room. Her head started to pound so
fiercely she bent over the sofa with the intention of ripping the telephone cord from
the wall. Just as she was about to give the
black cord a good yank, the phone stopped
ringing. The silence was deafening in the
small room.

"Now, he'll probably make some remark
tomorrow that I was out partying all night
and what kind of editor am I?" she thought
nastily. She would agree if the subject came
up. It was none of his business what she did
or where she went. Why was she getting so
hyper? She didn't even know if it was Teak
Helm. But it had to be him. People, as a
rule, were considerate of others and didn't

call after ten o'clock unless it was an emergency. She knew it wasn't her father because he had the manager's number downstairs, and he would have had her come up and tell her any bad news. No, it had to be Teak Helm.

Cathy munched her way through the wedge of cheese and attacked the tiny wheat thin crackers. Just as she picked up the tea cup the phone shrilled again. The tea splashed over the rim and soaked into her robe. Everyone knew it was almost impossible to get tea stains out of something white. She was angry now, angry at her own clumsiness and angry at the noisy phone.

Her movements were savage when she scooped up the ebony receiver and placed it next to her ear. Her voice was cold, defying anything, save a civil hello on the other end. "Catherine Bissette please," said a nasally voice. Two rapid sneezes in succession followed.

"This is Catherine Bissette."

"Teak Helm here. I realize the hour is late, but I've been trying to reach you all evening and there's been no answer. One second please." Cathy waited, drawing in her breath, and listened to more sneezing and a hacking cough that sounded like gravel being pushed through a grinder. Liar, she wanted to shout, I've been here all night, but she remained quiet, remembering Mr. Denuvue's words of caution. "I received your...suggestions some time ago, but as you can hear, I've been laid up with pneumonia. I was discharged from the hospital today, and this is the first chance I've had to call you."

Cathy waited, hardly daring to breathe. What was he going to say about the revisions? Aside from the heavy cold he didn't sound like such an ogre.

"I'm willing to make several concessions," Teak Helm said. "I have a busy day tomorrow, so why don't we just go over them now?"

"Do you realize what time it is, Mr. Helm?"

"Only too well. If you had been home earlier, we could have resolved this matter by seven thirty. Now, write this down because I won't go over it again."

"Very well, Mr. Helm. I'm waiting," Cathy said tartly.

"I know what time it is and you've no doubt been partying all evening and have no desire to do this, but I don't much care at the moment. I, myself, don't feel all that well. Now on page sixty-six I agree to the change. On page one hundred forty-three the situation has been changed, and as you'll see, the outcome is the way you want. That's it."

Cathy gasped. "But that's only two changes. What about the rest of my suggestions? Mr. Helm, I'm only trying to help you make a decent book great. All the ingredients are there, but the spirit is lacking. In short, Mr. Helm, your lead character is peripheral at best. He has no depth. Your readers are going to be disappointed," Cathy begged, seeing her dream of a revised manuscript going down the drain.

Teak Helm sneezed again, this time not bothering to hold the receiver away from his mouth. "Why don't you let me worry about my readers and just stick to your job?"

"You are my job. And you're right about one thing, you had better worry about your readers, because once they read this book they're going to know it's far from your best. Let me say that I've read each and every one of your books and this one doesn't compare to your first one in anyway, shape or form. Did you hear me, Mr. Helm, there's no spirit of sea adventure in this manuscript at all. Since you're writing sea adventures, it might behoove you to at least give me the courtesy of listening to me. I was looking forward to a long and lasting working relationship.''

"If that's your intent, then I suggest you do what I tell you. I corrected the galleys and followed the two suggestions of yours that I agreed with. I have no desire to withhold my manuscript that is due the day after tomorrow. In short, Miss Bissette, if you persist in trying to sway me to your way of thinking I may not deliver the manuscript at all. Do we understand each other?''

"Perfectly, Mr. Helm. I just have one question. If I was a man and made the same suggestions, would you have considered them?''

"Thinking of burning your bra, Miss Bissette?"

Cathy sputtered trying to find the proper words. She looked at the receiver in her hand and then replaced it with a loud bang, but not before she heard a loud and lusty sneeze.

"I hope you choke to death," Cathy snarled to the phone. Why in all the world did she have to come across two obnoxious men as Teak Helm and Jared Parsons? They must have been whipped up from the same mold. She wouldn't cry; she was beyond tears. She had done her best and it wasn't good enough. Tomorrow she would tell Mr. Denuvue that she would finish out the week and then leave. She'd go back to Swan Quarter where she belonged. New York and all its polished apples could function without her. Who needs it?

Two changes and he acted as if he was doing her a favor. And to top it off, threaten not to deliver the new manuscript. And what business was it of his if she partied all night long? And to lie on top of that and say he had been trying to call her all night long. That business about the hospital. She just bet he was in the hospital. Hospitals didn't discharge patients that sounded like he did. Who did he think he was fooling; she knew a death rattle when she heard it.

Dejectedly, she climbed into bed and lay in the dark, her eyes dry. She should cry; maybe she would feel better. No, she was all grown up now, and she had shed all her tears back in Swan Quarter. She had botched it up and tomorrow she was going to march in to Walter Denuvue's office, confess and then hand in her resignation. But the tears she held in check trickled down her cheeks while she slept.

Chapter Nine

When Cathy woke in the morning, no one was more surprised than herself to see her back stiff and her shoulders squared. She wasn't going to resign; she had never been a quitter and she wasn't quitting now. They would have to tie her and bundle her up and then ship her out in the late afternoon mail before she would depart Harbor House Publishing. She would dig in and fight to the last ditch. The only thing she would be guilty of was trying to help a good author become a great author. Somehow or other he slid off the track on this last book, and if there was a way to get him back on, she would do it. Please God, she prayed silently, don't let Mr. Denuvue fire me. Not yet anyway.

The moment Cathy walked into the office she knew something was different. The other editors were looking at her with a mixture of awe and something that looked like naked embarrassment. Billy was staring at her with blank eyes, waiting for her to walk to her desk. Walter Denuvue himself was exiting his office, both arms outstretched. "How nice of you to get here early, Cathy, we've all been waiting to see what's in there," he said, motioning to her desk.

Cathy wet her dry lips and gaped at the area where Mr. Denuvue was pointing. A meadow of wild flowers blanketed her desk and chair. Propped in the middle of the garden of color was a manila envelope bearing Teak Helm's stamp.

Overwhelmed with what met her eyes, Cathy found it hard to open the yellow envelope. Her eyes scanned the printed words on the slip of paper. A wicked smile played around the corners of her mouth. She handed the slip of paper to Walter Denuvue who grinned. "You did it, Cathy. You brought Teak Helm around. Good girl," he said, patting her on the shoulder. "What else is in the envelope?"

"The two revisions he originally agreed to do. Do you believe it, Mr. Denuvue, Teak Helm has actually agreed to all, not just a few, but all of my suggestions. Walter," she said, reverting to his first name, "this is going to be such a grand book when we're finished, his best to date. I'm so excited. You're not going to believe this, but last night when I went to bed I made up my mind that I was going to resign this morning. I was so sure after my conversation with Mr. Helm last evening that he would never, under any circumstances, come around to my way of thinking. I wonder what made him change his mind."

"Your charm, of course," Walter said magnanimously. "Right now, I think the most pressing problem of the day is what to do with this botanical garden."

"Walter, can't I keep them?" Cathy asked in a little girl voice. "I never saw so many wild flowers in my life. In fact, this is the first time a man ever sent me flowers.''

''Of course, you can keep them,'' Walter answered gruffly. ''Billy! Help Cathy move these wonders of nature so she can find her desk, but be careful, the petals bruise easily.''

Cathy hardly noticed the day pass until her phone rang shortly before four o'clock. A cool, aloof voice informed her that her name was Megan White and she was Mr. Helm's secretary. ''Mr. Helm wishes me to advise you that we are working around the clock to follow your suggestions. Someone from the office will check in with you every day to advise you of our progress.''

Cathy was too stunned to utter more than a cursory, ''Fine,'' and hang up the receiver.

The balance of the week passed, to Cathy's surprise, with a manila envelope arriving each morning, bearing the current revisions. Walter, if he noticed that the new manuscript was overdue, made no mention of it to Cathy, who was only too aware of the fact. Was all of this a blind of some sort?

Was Teak Helm doing as she asked and was he then going to jam down Walter's throat that the house was in breach of contract or some such nonsense? He had never been late before on delivery. Was he going to go somewhere else with his book? Would she be blamed? She couldn't think of that now. For now she had to concentrate on the manuscript in her hand. Another three days, if Teak kept working at his present speed, and the manuscript could go. And go it would. It was the best, surely he could see that. And if Walter could light a fire under his promotion staff and have the book billed as his best yet and give it the proper promotion, then it would take off like a rocket. Personally, she loved it, from the first page to the last, and Teak was sticking strictly to her suggestions, neither adding nor deleting, doing exactly what she had outlined. She wondered vaguely how his cold was. She wondered other things too; like why did a different secretary call her every day? Did men like Teak Helm surround themselves with gorgeous girls who posed as secretaries like Jared Parsons had with Erica? The last secretary hadn't sounded too bright when she said, "Mr. Helm doesn't mind a whit if y'all take a few liberties with his words."

"I wouldn't think of it," Cathy had replied.

"Well, feel free, Sugar. Mr. Helm don't mind at all."

Friday afternoon arrived and so did another delivery of flowers from the florist. This time it was a colossal arrangement of multicolored daisies, Cathy's favorite flower. Gathering together her belongings, she made her way past Walter's office, the flowers held aloft like a beacon. Cathy grinned and rang for the elevator. The first thing she was going to do when she got home was call her father and tell him of her weeks' trials and of the flowers. Then she was going to wash her hair and clean her apartment. Her world was right side up and she loved it. Perhaps it still tilted slightly but good enough for now. Lucas was certainly going to be surprised about Helm's revisions on the galleys. Her heart fluttered like a trapped bird when she imagined that Lucas' first words would be news of Jared Parsons. First, she would start off by asking about Bizzy, that was always good for fifteen minutes. Another five to catch up on Lucas' health, which was always fine, and then the nonchalant question about Jared. But only if her father didn't volunteer news.

Cathy waited impatiently as the phone rang in Swan Quarter. Four, five, six. "Hello," came the harried greeting.

"Dad. How are you?"

"Fine, and you?"

"Just fine. How's Bizzy?"

"Fine. He's out on the strip pretending that he's going to catch a fish any minute now. How's your new job progressing?" Lucas asked casually.

"Dad, you won't believe what I'm going to tell you, but I'm going to tell you anyway. Teak Helm came around to my way of thinking and has agreed to all of my suggested revisions. Dad, he sent me a whole carload of wild flowers a few days after I took over as his editor, and just today, a florist delivered a gigantic bouquet of daisies. It's the first time a man ever sent me flowers," she babbled, "and we've never even met. Actually, I just spoke to him on the phone once, and at that time he said it was going to be his way or not at all. I was going to resign in the morning, but sometime during the night he must have had a change of heart and decided I knew what I was talking about. There is one other little problem, however. His new manuscript hasn't arrived and I'm beginning to worry. Though Mr. Denuvue isn't concerned. I think! But we're all very careful not to mention it, hoping it will arrive in the next mail.''

''It sounds like you're back in the swing of things. By the way, I mailed you a package the other day; it should be waiting for you in the mailbox.''

''What did you send?'' Cathy asked curiously, thinking she had left something behind.

Lucas laughed. ''I sent you a very old book.'' He laughed again. ''My prize possession. Lefty Rudder's novel, *The Sea Gypsy.*''

''Dad, you didn't! Why?''

''I just thought you might like to have it since you're so involved with your Teak

Helm sea adventures. Read it over and see
how they compare.''

Cathy's tone was puzzled. ''But, Dad, I've
read that book. A long time ago, as a matter
of fact.''

''That's why I want you to read it again.
Now that you're grown up,'' Lucas said
dryly.

''Do you want a book report?'' Cathy
asked just as dryly.

''A phone call will do if it isn't too much
trouble.''

Cathy ignored his tone this time and
wished there was some way she could tact-
fully ask about Jared Parsons. She decided
to throw caution to the wind and bluntly ask
outright. ''Did you finish the repairs on Mr.
Parsons' boat?''

''Sure did and he's gone.''

''Oh,'' Cathy said, trying to hide her dis-
appointment. Wasn't he going to say anything else? No, he was going to make her
ask. ''Have you seen Erica what's-her-name
again?''

''As a matter of fact, I did see her. I drove
her to the airport the day after the Fourth of

July picnic. She went back to New York, a big modeling assignment was what she said. Something about her perfect skin being just right for this new cosmetic that's being advertised.''

Cathy's heart pounded and then settled down to a dull throbbing. Then she hadn't been in seclusion on the yacht with Jared for three days as she had originally thought. Her voice was light when she spoke again. ''Really?''

''Yes, really. Now don't you feel ashamed for all those nasty suspicions?''

''Not really,'' Cathy laughed.

''Cat, I hope you don't mind, but I gave Jared your address and phone number. He said he was going to be in New York for a while. And he said he would like to take you out to dinner. I thought you would enjoy it.''

''Dad, don't lie to me. Did he ask or did you volunteer?'' Cathy asked, holding her breath, waiting for his answer.

''I'm not even going to bother answering that question. I thought children were supposed to get smarter the older they got. I guess that means he hasn't called you.

Probably changed his mind. He should have called by now.''

Lucas' tone was almost petulant, making Cathy grin. Serves you right; fathers shouldn't meddle in their grown daughters' affairs. "Guess so," Cathy said airily. "If you say Erica is here modeling then we can both understand why he hasn't called, can't we, Dad?"

It was evident to Cathy from the lack of response that Lucas had not considered that particular possibility. "All I can tell you is he said he was going to look you up. Parsons is a man of his word and I, for one, believe him. He probably hasn't caught up on his business.''

"Don't worry, Dad, I can handle it, and if I run into any trouble, I'll give you a call.''

"Are you eating right and getting enough sleep?'' Lucas asked, making it sound like an afterthought, not knowing how to end the conversation.

Cathy giggled. "Tonight I'm having Chicken Kiev with green salad. I picked up some fresh corn-on-the-cob yesterday at the market, and for dessert I'm whipping up a peach cobbler. After I gorge myself I'm going to retire, which should be around eight o'clock," she fibbed, allaying his concern.

"I'm having left-over lamb stew," Lucas said wistfully. "Goodbye, Cat."

Cathy shrugged. She wished she had some of the stew he was talking about.

Her hair rolled into a thick turkish towel, Cathy placed her frozen dinner into a pot of boiling water and watched the plastic bag settle to the top. She shrugged. Chinese food had long been a favorite of hers, and she even had a fortune cookie tucked away in the kitchen cabinet to make the dinner complete.

While the Chinese dinner bubbled merrily in the pot, Cathy took a quick bracing shower and then wrapped herself in a faded flannel robe that had seen too many washings.

The table was set with her solitary plate and silverware, the luxurious vase of daisies making the table look festive. Carefully, she scooped out the contents of the boil bag onto her plate and placed the fortune cookie at the top of her plate. A bottle of beer and a glass were added as she sat down. The first forkful was poised in midair when her door bell rang. Must be the landlady with her mail. Chewing enthusiastically, she opened the door and gulped the food she was chewing. Her eyes widened and then her face drained of all color. "He...hello, Jared," she managed squeakily. Of all the tacky luck.

"Are you coming or going?" Jared grinned.

"Well...I was...actually...come in," Cathy said, holding the door wide for him to enter. Her mouth was dry, making it difficult to swallow as she watched Jared's eyes rake the room and come to rest on her solitary dinner. Certainly, this could only compare to a hovel in his eyes, she thought defensively.

"Do you like my daisies?" she asked pertly. Why should she care if he did or didn't like her apartment, she was the one who paid the rent.

"A bit much, I think," Jared said coolly.

"Well, I happen to love them, and I don't think they're a bit much. I think the bouquet is just right. Teak Helm sent them to me," she said smugly.

"I think I understand," Jared answered. "The simple things in life please you, like this small apartment and the field daisies. I really didn't mean to interrupt your dinner, I just stopped by to ask if you would care to go to dinner with me on Tuesday."

Cathy's face flamed, knowing full well where he had been spending his days. Erica. Erica must be busy, why else would he be looking her up? "Fine," she said happily. Erica's loss would be her gain. "Where?"

"Where what?" Jared asked, puzzled.

"Where will we go for dinner? It would help if I knew, so I can dress accordingly."

"Forgive me, yes, I see what you mean. I was thinking of something else. I'm sorry."

"You said that twice, that you're sorry." Cathy frowned. This certainly wasn't the Jared she knew back in Swan Quarter.

Jared ignored the comment. "Are daisies really your favorite flower?" he asked, then continued. "We'll go to the restaurant by Central Park. I'm sorry that your dinner is cold. I'll make it up to you on Tuesday."

Before she knew what was happening, Jared had the door opened and was gone. He hadn't said goodbye and he had made no move to kiss her, and, most important of all, he hadn't made fun of her. Strange, she thought, I think I liked him better the old way. Maybe it was a trick of some sort and he was going to spring some dastardly trick on her at the eleventh hour—like having her get all dressed up and then stand her up. It sounded stupid and Cathy was glad she hadn't said it aloud even though there was no one to hear.

Gingerly, she sat down on the wrought iron chair at the table and stared at the mass of white and yellow daisies. Idly, she picked a bloom and started to peel the petals. He loves me, he loves me not. He loves me not! Cathy dropped the last petal as though it was a scorching brand. Only children played that game. She picked another bloom—he loves me, he loves me not. He loves me not! Best out of three, she muttered, her dinner forgotten. He loves me, he loves me not. He loves me! Who? Teak Helm, the flower giver, or Jared Parsons? Jared Parsons, of course. She didn't even know Teak Helm.

Cathy glanced at her watch as she cleared the table. If she hurried she could keep her word and be in bed by eight o'clock. Since dinner was a fiasco, she would at least not be a complete liar. First, she would have to go downstairs to get her mail.

Don't think about Jared Parsons, she scolded herself; if you do, you'll spend another sleepless night. Let it be enough that he came by and invited you personally rather than use a phone. As she scraped her cold dinner into the garbage disposal, she noticed that her hands were trembling, and she knew her cheeks were flushed.

After gathering her mail and slipping back into her apartment, Cathy slid the chain and the bolt on her apartment door. She turned off the two burning lamps and returned to her room.

It was ten minutes to four when Cathy laid down the book her father sent her and stared at the bedside clock. It wasn't possible. It just wasn't possible that her beloved Teak Helm would stop short of plagiarizing the famous Lefty Rudder. That's why Lucas had sent the book. He wanted her to see with her own eyes. There had to be an explanation. There just had to be.

Why did she feel so betrayed? So wounded? Oh, what was she to do now? Could she ignore it, give the man a warning via one of his secretaries, or should she go to Walter Denuvue and give him the book Lucas sent along with the galleys. Why were all these things happening to her? Did she wear some invisible sign that said, "Dump on Cathy Bissette!" I know there is some explanation that will clear up all of this. I know it! Tears smarted in her eyes as she slid beneath the covers. It seemed like the whole world was crumbling about her. Would Jared Parsons stay around long enough to pick up the pieces?

Cathy sat bolt upright, a stunned look on her face. Her eyes were wide as she stared about the room, a wild look in her eyes. "I love him, I love Jared Parsons!"

Chapter Ten

The weekend passed in a blur for Cathy who alternated between bouts of depression and non-stop eating binges. Sleep was something to dream about, and every bone in her body was weary because of her endless pacing. Monday morning seemed an eternity away. When it did arrive, Cathy was thankful even though there was a steady downpour that greeted her when she exited her apartment building. It suited her, gray and damp. By the time she reached the office her shoes were sodden and her hair hung about her face in damp ringlets, making her look like a winsome child of twelve.

Finding a note on Walter Denuvue's door that said he was not going to be in till Wednesday set Cathy into a near frenzy. Now, what was she going to do? There was no one to talk to, no one to complain to, no one to tell her what to do. She always seemed to be alone when it mattered most.

Cathy sat at her desk for what seemed like an hour before she picked up the phone to dial the number Teak Helm's secretary had given her. Quickly and concisely, she stated her problem, ending with, "I must speak with Mr. Helm, it's imperative." She listened a moment to the cool voice on the other end of the phone. "Very well, Miss White, if Mr. Helm is not available then please tell him I would like to speak with him about the word plagiarism and what it means. As soon as possible." The squeal on the other end of the phone made Cathy rear back as she pulled the receiver from her ear.

"Are you saying Mr. Helm plagiarized someone?" came the excited squeal.

Cathy was fed up, fed up with Teak Helm and his unavailability. Privacy was one thing, but his insulation, provided by his secretaries, was something else. In his own way, the famous writer was as bad as Jared Parsons, who was still an enigma to her. Cut from the same mold, she sniffed. Her voice was cool, almost verging on ice, when she spoke, "The word, Miss White, means whatever Mr. Helm wants it to mean. I'll be in the office till three and then I'm leaving. If Mr. Helm wants to talk to me, tell him to call me before then or at the office tomorrow. I do not conduct business from my home, be sure to explain that to him."

"Goodness gracious, honey, don't go getting yourself all stirred up. I'll pass along your message to Mr. Helm, but in the meantime why don't you just explain it all in writing and send it along?"

Cathy didn't bother to reply. What was the use? Her head was beginning to ache, and she had a long day to get through, but she meant it when she said she was leaving at three. She was going shopping to buy a new dress for her night on the town with Jared Parsons. Teak Helm could just go fly a kite for all she cared. She had done all she could under the circumstances.

The morning passed uneventfully. Dutifully, Cathy picked at a tuna sandwich at her desk and drank cup after cup of strong, black coffee. It was three o'clock and still no word from Teak Helm. Plus she had gone through the mail and all the messenger deliveries and there was still no new manuscript bearing the Teak Helm stamp. Her movements were sure and very precise when she covered her typewriter. She dusted off her desk with a Kleenex and then sharpened her pencils. She picked up a stray paper clip and tossed it into a tattered box sitting on her desk. She didn't like the way the rubber bands were spilling out of another small box, so she straightened them and then sat down. It was 3:10. So much for Teak Helm caring about what she thought. If he dared to call her at home tonight, she would simply hang up on him. If he couldn't give her the courtesy of talking with her during office hours, she certainly owed him nothing. Who did he think he was anyway? She was leaving!

Nothing pleased her in the department stores; nothing pleased her in the small boutiques. She picked and rejected; this color wasn't right; this style made her look too young; this one made her look like a matron and always she looked for something like Erica would wear. When it dawned on her what she was doing, she settled down to serious shopping for herself, Cathy Bissette. A simple, pale lavender linen was her final choice. With a deeper shade of lavender at the throat by way of a scarf, along with a deep purple braided belt, she felt she could hold her own.

Cathy's eyes sparkled when the salesgirl rang up the amount. It was outrageous, sinful, to spend so much money on one dress. Yet she paid it happily.

To take a taxi or not was now the question. Definitely not, the cost of the dress would probably haunt her for days to come, and the thirteen block walk wouldn't hurt her. She barely noticed the pouring rain, and she sloshed her way home, the expensive dress clutched next to her breast in the plastic shopping bag.

As the long evening wore on, she found herself wishing the phone would ring just so she could tell Teak Helm what she thought of him. She suffered along with the heroine through a two hour movie and then switched off the television only to turn it back on and watch the news. She might as well wait till after midnight before going to bed. Teak Helm didn't seem to have much regard for time. The last time he had called her at midnight. She wasn't going to sleep anyway.

The newswoman reporting the day's events finally put her to sleep. When she woke, it was four-thirty in the morning, and her shoulders ached from sleeping in an awkward position. She yawned and made her way to her bed.

The note on her desk Tuesday morning did not lighten her mood. So, he didn't have the nerve to talk to her. "Hrumph," she snorted as she ripped open the envelope. The sentence was short, curt, almost obscene, in its shortness. "This time you're wrong," she read aloud. The signature was nothing more than a scrawl.

Cathy's eyes raked the office. "I refuse to become angry; I will not scream and yell. I will not cry. I realize there are perfect people in the world, of which I am not one. I will remain sensible and calm and wait for Mr. Denuvue to return and then dump this on him." Dramatically, she dusted her hands together to show she had enough. Already she felt better. "Out of sight, out of mind, Mr. Helm," she muttered to herself as she rolled a piece of paper into her typewriter. Quickly, she dashed off a short note to Lucas bringing him up to date and explaining that she would not be making any calls for a while till she made up for buying her expensive dress for her date tonight. Carefully, she avoided any mention that Jared Parsons was her date. Just as she ripped the paper from the machine, her phone rang. Megan White, Teak Helm's secretary, inquiring if Miss Bissette had received his letter.

Cathy sucked in her breath. "But, of course," she purred, "messengers are most prompt."

"And...?" Megan White asked curiously.

"And nothing." Chew on that for a while, Cathy thought nastily. "Tell me," she asked curiously, "how do you stand working for such a perfect person?"

A small chuckle warmed Cathy's ear. Gone was the dumb, demure Southern drawl. "It ain't easy. The pay is terrific and the fringe benefits are great. Do you have a message for Mr. Helm?''

Cathy thought for a minute and then grinned. "But, of course, tell Mr. Helm to sit on it!''

"Gotcha. Verbatim, right?''

"You got it.''

The moment Cathy replaced the receiver her world was right side up. For the first time since returning from Swan Quarter she felt in control. She had solved her problem, and she had a date with a man she was in love with. What could be better? The sun was shining and she felt terrific. As a matter of fact, she felt great.

Cathy sailed through the rest of the day smiling at one and all. Her mood seemed to transfer itself to the other girls, and before she knew it they were all laughing and talking, but working at break-neck speed to finish so they too could leave early.

Cathy's heart thumped in her chest at the sound of the door bell. Should she wait for it to ring a second time? Nonsense, she couldn't wait to feast her eyes on the handsome Jared Parsons. She wanted to throw her arms around him and crush him to her. Instead, she stepped aside and didn't fail to notice the approving look in his eye. It was worth every cent she paid for the dress. More, I'd have paid twice that amount she said to herself.

"I see you're ready. I like that. I don't appreciate waiting around for a woman to powder her nose," Jared said with a twinkle in his eye.

Seated in the restaurant, Cathy felt strangely relaxed in Jared's company. Cathy sipped at her Marguerita while Jared drank his Scotch as though he were dying of thirst. He finished it and ordered another. "I had a rough day," he offered by way of explanation.

"Really. I had a wonderful day," Cathy confided happily. "I solved a problem and I no longer have the weight of the world on my shoulders. To put it more simply, I no longer care."

Jared placed his drink on the table with what Cathy considered deliberate movement. "Tell me about your day. Tell me what you do at that office of yours."

Cathy stared deeply into Jared's eyes and suddenly wanted him to know everything there was to know about Cathy Bissette. "I work as an editor for Harbor House Publishing. I was just made Mr. Helm's editor. Don't be impressed. It's nothing more than a glorified title. He's an insufferable man. He actually had the gall to call me at home one evening and expected me to believe he had just been released from the hospital and that's why he was calling so late. He doesn't appear to have any concern or consideration for anyone. He told me straight out that he was not going to make any changes in his manuscript. You see, I felt the novel was wrong, all the spirit was gone from his writing, and I didn't want him to cheat his readers. Somehow or other, he got off the track on this particular book. I was objective, at least I thought I was, when I made suggestions. The following morning Mr. Helm sent me a garden of wild flowers along with two of the revisions that I suggested, saying he would follow all of my suggestions. But," Cathy said, holding up a warning finger, "he had a manuscript that was due in two days and so far it still hasn't arrived. I'm afraid that he may not deliver. You see, Jared, if Mr. Helm goes to another publisher, Harbor House Publishing would go bankrupt. The Teak Helm novels are keeping the house going. A lot of people would be out of work, some of them elderly who aren't quite ready to retire yet. They could never get another job." She was breathless when she finished speaking. She gulped at her drink, wishing she hadn't said so much.

"You sound like you don't care for Mr. Helm very much. Why did you take on the job? And what makes you doubt the fact that the man said he just got out of the hospital?"

"I don't know Mr. Helm. I only spoke to him that one time. All of our contact has been through the mail or through his secretaries. He is the most unavailable, insulated man I've ever had the misfortune not to meet. I doubt that he was in the hospital because no self-respecting doctor would release someone who was coughing and sputtering the way he was on the phone. He sounded terribly sick. I guess what I don't understand is why a man as famous as Teak Helm needs all this privacy; it's almost like he's hiding out. Maybe he's afraid of people. I don't know what his problem is, and right now I care less."

Jared's tone was soft, intimate, when he spoke. "And what problem did you eliminate today?"

"I eliminated Teak Helm," Cathy said, smoothly sipping at her second drink. She was going to have to watch it, she was beginning to feel giddy. "You see," she said, leaning over the table to stare at Jared, "my father sent me..." why were Jared's eyes so flinty? "...sent me an old book written a long time ago by Lefty Rudder. Did Dad tell you Lefty Rudder used to be one of his closest friends? Well, anyway, I read it over last night, and would you believe, could you believe, that Mr. Helm has plagiarized an adventure right out of the pages of Lefty Rudder's *Sea Gypsy?*" She waited expectantly for Jared's comment, and when it came, she was disappointed.

"That's a very serious accusation, Cathy. Who else have you told?" Jared asked smoothly, yet there was an intensity behind his words.

"Mr. Denuvue is out of town, but I certainly will tell him tomorrow morning when he returns," Cathy said adamantly.

"Do you always treat a man's good name so carelessly, Miss Bissette?"

"Of course not. I sent him a letter as his secretary requested and I made a copy for the records. Mr. Helm replied that I was wrong and that was the end of it." Her heart plummeted at the formal sound of Miss Bissette. She shouldn't have told him. She bristled at his piercing look. "Look, Jared, my first obligation is to my publisher," Cathy said, waving her arm in the air and coming to rest on the table. She suddenly felt out of her depth with Jared's gaze on her and, as usual, she made a clumsy move, knocking over her drink. Aghast, she drew in her breath at the stain on the snowy tablecloth.

A wry smile played around the corners of Jared's mouth. "I trust you can handle the matter in your own graceful style," he said smoothly, looking pointedly at the tablecloth. She had done it again!

When they arrived at the restaurant Cathy was amazed at how quickly Jared could put awkward conversation behind him and go on as though nothing had happened. Unfortunately, Cathy felt strained and she kept her eyes lowered while she ate, answering only when Jared asked her a pointed question. She knew she was being childish, and yet she couldn't look into his eyes, fearful that she would in some way give away her feelings.

She heard Jared sigh. He was fed up with her attitude, she could tell. "Cathy, look at me," Jared commanded. Obediently, she raised her head and stared at the man across the table from her. "What's wrong, why can't you enjoy yourself when you're in my company?"

Cathy swallowed hard. "I feel very uncomfortable around you. It's not a bad feeling; it's a feeling that somehow or other you're going to... what I mean is I am very aware of you and how you make me feel. I won't lie to you. I'm not quite as sophisticated as your secretary and the other women you must have known... know. These feelings are rather alien to me. Oh, I've gone out with other men and was almost engaged at the beginning of summer, but I changed my mind. He just wasn't a person I felt I wanted to spend the rest of my life with."

Jared smiled. "What kind of man would you like to spend the rest of your life with?"

Cathy smiled too at his words. "Someone like you, perhaps, but only after I got to know you better," she said honestly.

Jared pushed back his chair and came to stand next to her. "I think," he said softly, "that this is as good a time as any for you to get to know me better." He held the chair for her. His touch on her arm was like wild fire. "I'm going to take you for a hansom ride through the park. Would you like that?"

"Jared, I would love it. I've lived in New York for two years, and I've never had a hansom ride through the park," she cried delightedly. "How wonderful of you to think of something like that."

"I have a confession to make. I come to New York at least four times a year and I've never done it either." He was like a little boy, Cathy thought, caught up in her excitement.

It was a summer night to remember. The air was kissed with the promise of fall, and the sky was black as velvet. There was almost an air of celebration, and the sidewalk strollers seemed enveloped in a conspiracy of the romantic night.

Jared hailed a cab and gave the driver instructions. Then he settled back against the seat, sitting close to her. She was sensitive to him, aware of him, liking the aroma of his cologne and the pressure of his shoulder against hers.

Like two children, they ran from the taxi and raced to the hansom cab. Jared helped her into the old-fashioned carriage, and when the driver flicked the reins and the horse obliged to his command, Cathy and Jared settled back into their seat and caught their breaths.

Central Park revealed its magic as they took the winding paths at an easy pace, and when Jared slipped his arm around her as though it was the most natural gesture in the world, Cathy knew the gentle happiness of being with the man she loved.

Down through the dark arches created by the overhanging trees, over quaint little bridges that were barred to traffic, they rode. Jared inhaled deeply. "It's almost like a different world, isn't it?"

Cathy nodded in agreement, not daring to say a word that would break the magic spell. Jared's arm tightened around her, bringing her head to nestle on his shoulder. She could feel his lips against her hair and then trail along her temple.

"You're a very special girl, Cathy Bissette, and I like being with you." The sound of his voice sent tremors up her spine.

Gently, as though he were afraid she would break, he turned her in his arms. "I'm going to kiss you, Cathy, because a girl like you should be kissed on a romantic evening like this, riding through Central Park in a hansom. But most of all, I'm going to kiss you because at this moment it's what I want most in this world. I've been watching you all evening: the way your eyes sparkle and change from blue to green; the way your mouth smiles and a tiny dimple shows just at the corner, there," he touched her mouth with the tip of his finger. "But, it's you I'll be kissing, Cathy, the woman you are. Not because I think you're beautiful on the outside, but because I know how beautiful you are in here," his hand fell to her chest, just below her throat.

Gently, with a tenderness that made her heart ache, he lowered his head and pressed his mouth to hers. Sparks ignited inside her head and burst into a flame that danced through her veins. A voice within repeated his name, Jared, Jared.

This was all Cathy wanted, all she needed. Any and all questions that had plagued her concerning him vanished. There was nothing else to know beyond this; Jared Parsons was the man she loved and she wanted to spend the rest of her life with him. She didn't care who he was or what he was, knowing in her heart that he could only be all things good and wonderful. And when the day came that he wanted to answer her silent questions, she would listen, knowing she had been right about him all along.

Cathy was the first one in the office, or so she thought, until she noticed Walter Denuvue on the phone. She motioned through the glass that she wanted to speak to him, and he waved at her, motioning for her to sit and wait in the small reception area. Seething and fuming, the Lefty Rudder novel in one hand and the Teak Helm galleys in the other, she paced the confines of the waiting area. The longer she waited, the angrier she became. The moment she saw Walter hang up the phone, she was through the door. Her voice was almost incoherent as she rushed to explain what was going on. Midway through her explanation she became aware of Walter's still impassive features. He was too calm, too unruffled. He didn't care! He really didn't care! She stopped and stared at the publisher, waiting.

"Cathy, don't concern yourself."

"Mr. Denuvue," she said formally, "I can't believe you said what you just said to me. How can you sit there and tell me not to concern myself over a case of plagiarism. It's here, in black and white. Teak Helm lifted this adventure right out of Lefty Rudder's sea adventure. He didn't steal words, he was too clever for that. He stole a creative idea and didn't even have the decency to do a good job with it. I quit!" she cried dramatically. "I'm going back to Swan Quarter where people know what decency and integrity are all about. I'm ashamed of you, Mr. Denuvue, not that you care, but I am. I'm ashamed of people like Teak Helm too. I don't want to be a party to any of this. Consider this my notice.''

Walter Denuvue lit his pipe, his eyes and voice unconcerned. ''Cathy, you have two weeks vacation left. You won't have to give notice. You can leave today if you'd like.'' Cathy clenched her jaw to keep her mouth from dropping open. Walter was so cool, so confident; this was not at all what she had expected. And to be dismissed so easily, it was insulting!

''If that's the way you feel about it, Walter, then that's exactly what I'll do. I'd rather shrimp for a living and get callouses on my hands for an honest day's work and eat the fruits of my labor. At least I won't get indigestion and heartburn, not to mention heartsick. I feel sorry for you, Walter, I thought you were a man of principle and that you knew what the word integrity meant.''

Walter shrugged. ''And take that damn pasture of flowers with you. I'm certainly not going to water them.''

Cathy stared at the publisher. ''You keep them, Walter. Mr. Helm made a mistake when he sent them to me; you should have been the one to receive them. I can't be bought," she said bitterly.

It took Cathy exactly seventeen and one half minutes to clear her desk and leave the office. No one paid any attention to her, and she was in no mood to explain anything to anyone. The ride down in the elevator was slow and she felt nothing. Her brief career in publishing was at an end.

Cathy spent the remainder of the day packing her belongings into cartons to be taken with her back to Swan Quarter. She would rent a car rather than ship her belongings. This way she could take her time on the long trip, staying over one night in a motel. It was funny, she thought, she would get home around the same time her letter reached her father. Wouldn't he be surprised that he was now going to have a permanent hand on the trawler? As far as she could tell, the only thing she was leaving behind was her Blue Cross insurance. Jared! Her heart lurched and then stilled. He didn't live in New York, and he said he only came to the city four times a year. Well, if he ever decided he wanted to see her, he would know where to find her.

Tonight he was taking her to a concert in the park. He certainly was big on outdoor dates. Or was he a romantic at heart? Would he kiss her tonight? What did he think of her now that she had been so brutally honest with him concerning her feelings? Probably nothing, she answered herself. He had time to kill while he was in New York and, no doubt, in his own way was taking her out because he figured he was doing Lucas a favor by doing so. Take out Lucas' daughter to show he was grateful for the fine work Lucas had done on his yacht. Whatever it was, she had made up her mind to enjoy it for what it was and ask no questions. When he went away, she would handle it, and in her mind was sure she would be the best person for having experienced it.

Cathy pulled a calendar from the desk drawer and made up her mind to leave on Saturday. This way she wouldn't have to rush. She made a list of things she had to do: leave forwarding address; have all the utilities turned off; transfer her small savings back to the bank in Swan Quarter; call the car rental company and reserve a car. Tell the landlady and thank her for not requiring a lease. If she did things in an orderly manner, she would have some time for a little leisurely shopping, perhaps a matinee or two and a little time left over for feeling sorry for herself.

Now, to tell Jared or not. No, she wasn't running away from him; she wasn't running away from anything. She was running to something. Home, the only home she had ever known. Swan Quarter was where she belonged, with or without Jared Parsons. Since she wasn't running away, there was no reason to tell Jared Parsons anything more about her business. When Saturday came, she would pack her belongings into the rental car and go home. It was as simple as that.

It was seven-thirty when her door bell rang, and Jared Parsons entered her apartment, fifteen minutes late. He offered no apologies but simply waited for her to get a sweater. They made small conversation in the elevator. The ride to Central Park was companionable and easy. Jared seemed to be enjoying her company. In a quiet voice he told her he loved music almost as much as he loved reading.

"That's right," Cathy said in some surprise. "You told me back in Swan Quarter that you were a fan of Teak Helm. And that you had read all of Lefty Rudder's novels also. You did say you preferred Teak Helm, didn't you?"

"Yes, I did. I find his novels very moving. I can almost envision myself in some of his scenes. To me, his characters are very alive."

"I wonder if you would have said that if you read his new novel before I made the suggested revisions. I wonder if you would have picked up, as a reader and fan, of course, the same lack of spirit I did."

Jared took his eyes from the road and stared at Cathy for a brief moment before returning to the traffic on the road. "I think I would have. I find that of late I'm a very critical reader. I'm not sure if that's good or bad. What do you think?"

"I think it's good, Jared. When a reader does that, it means the author has succeeded. Emotion, good or bad, is good. No two people read or look at anything in the same light. Do you understand what I'm saying?''

"Yes, I do. Tell me, has Mr. Helm's new manuscript arrived in the mail yet? Yesterday you said he was late.''

"I'm afraid not.'' Cathy curtailed further conversation on the matter by telling Jared to start watching for the entrance to the park. Diverted for the moment, Jared concentrated on the road. Cathy watched him out of the corner of her eye. The grim set of his strong jaw puzzled her. What was he thinking? Why did he have to be such an enigma? Did he feel anything about her? Surely, he must feel something, some small twinge of something.

It wasn't his tone that startled her but his words, almost as if he knew, "What kind of day did you have?''

"A difficult one,'' Cathy said shortly, remembering her decision not to tell Jared of her leaving Harbor House and her decision to go back to Swan Quarter. She didn't want to explain to anyone, not even Jared Parsons whom she loved. She knew in her heart he would have something wise, something smart to say. He would mock her with his eyes if not with words.

"That sounds rather terminal," Jared said coolly. Cathy's mind raced as did her heart. What did that statement mean? He couldn't know, could he? Of course not. How could he? A guilty conscience on her part. Why should she feel guilty about not telling him she resigned?

Jared parked the car with smooth expertise and cut the ignition. He turned to look at Cathy. "You didn't answer my question."

"I wasn't aware that you asked a question," Cathy said, flustered at his usual mocking tone. "All I remember you saying was it sounded terminal."

"Yes, that's what I said. Most people would make some sort of comment to a statement like that."

"I'm not like most people," Cathy said, climbing from the car.

"That's true," Jared grinned as he, too, climbed from the car and locked it. "I find you most refreshing, Cathy Bissette. I think I can truthfully say I've never met anyone quite like you."

Cathy couldn't help it. "And I've never met anyone quite like you. Some day, Jared Parsons, I would like to know what makes you tick."

His touch on her arm, as he walked next to her, was familiar, and Cathy savored the feel of it. She did love him. Couldn't he tell? Did he care? How could one person love another so much and not have that love returned? Would she ever know?

The concert was long and lovely and Cathy, relishing every minute of it, was sorry when it was over. Jared, too, seemed caught up in the music. He held her hand in companionable silence, and from time to time he squeezed it to show he was aware that she was next to him. He made no move to put his arms around her or to kiss her like the other couples were doing in the darkness. Cathy felt resentful of his aloofness, his calculated aloofness. She didn't know why she thought that but she did.

Jared double-parked outside her apartment building. She handed him her key, and he deftly opened the door with no fumbling or bumbling. Why did she always have to stand there for ten minutes till she made contact with the lock? He did everything without wasted motion. "Good night, Cathy," he said softly. "How would you like to go see a Broadway play with me tomorrow night? My broker gave me tickets and I thought you might enjoy it."

"I'd love to go," Cathy said simply and honestly. "Thank you for asking me."

"It's my pleasure, Cathy. I enjoy your company, and you're an easy person to be with. I'll pick you up around seven-thirty."

"I'll be ready. Good night, Jared," she said longingly, staring into his eyes, willing him to at least kiss her on the cheek. Instead, he smiled and waved nonchalantly and left, telling her to be sure to slide the bolt and slip the chain. She nodded mutely. Maybe tomorrow, she sighed, as she followed his instructions. In some ways he was just like her father.

Cathy spent a restless night, her fitful dreams invaded again by a tall, muscular man chasing her down the river bank. He resembled Jared Parsons in build, but his face was blank. In his hand he clutched a book. Cathy woke, her forehead beaded with perspiration. She was no dream analyst, but she knew the man chasing her was a mixture of Jared Parsons and Teak Helm, the two men responsible for turning her world topsy-turvy.

The bedroom drapes open to her satisfaction, Cathy lounged around the tiny room, picking up a knickknack here and putting it down. She made the bed with grim purpose, twisting and tugging at the rumpled sheets till she had them as tight as any boot camp recruit could make them. She fumbled in her purse for a quarter and watched it bounce off the tight covers. So what, she snarled to herself. It just goes to prove I know how to make a bed.

Why hadn't Jared kissed her last night? What was the point of all this formality? Was he trying to lull her into a false sense of security, and when she was unaware, he would spring. Men did that, they were always doing it in the movies. "Spring already," she shouted to the empty room. Tears gathered in her eyes and she made no move to hold them in check. Who was there to see or care for that matter if her eyes were red and swollen? Nobody.

Cathy fixed herself a sketchy breakfast, one Pop Tart and a cup of Chinese tea. She looked with revulsion at the blueberry tart that had burned in the toaster and then tossed it into the trash. The tea was weak and smelled terrible. So much for breakfast. Blowing her nose lustily in a paper towel, she sat down with a thump on the yellow kitchen chair. What was she going to do to while away her day? She wasn't fooling anyone, especially herself. Inside of an hour she could have all her belongings inside a cardboard carton and be on her way. Why was she dilly-dallying? Because of Jared Parsons, of course. And because she secretly hoped that somehow, someway, Teak Helm would get in touch with her. Once the telephone was turned off, it would put an end to such hope. She knew he wasn't going to call and admit to a thing. Walter Denuvue had made that very clear. So clear in fact, her ears were still ringing with his words.

What do to? Go to the World Trade Center. One last look at New York. Why not? She dressed and set out. She felt like she was going on a mission of sorts. The people she passed were a blur to her. She nodded to some and smiled at others. Cathy paid her admission and waited for the next elevator. It was a dramatic tribute to engineering, she thought. She should feel impressed but she wasn't. Carefully, she edged her way over to the long windows and looked out and then down. This was her last look at New York. Had she given anything? Was she leaving anything behind? What had New York given her? Was she taking anything back to Swan Quarter with her? She decided the answer was a draw. She had given nothing and she had taken nothing. She was free to go. Free to go home.

The elevator ride down seemed endless. Impatience now to get back to her apartment made her rush through the lobby and out to the street. Quickly, she hailed a cab, knowing she couldn't afford it but doing it anyway.

Her apartment looked the same; there were no messages on the foyer table and no mail. Her telephone was silent. She felt lost, forgotten.

For lunch she fixed herself a plate of crackers and cheese and a glass of apple juice. She forced herself to eat, the dry crackers sticking to the roof of her mouth. The cheese didn't appeal to her, and she left it sitting on the plate till it started to dry out along the edges.

Television might make her feel a little more alive. The actors and actresses on the "soaps" always had so many problems maybe she could identify with them for a little while. She watched several soap operas and sat through seven commercials till the four-thirty movie came on, then waited impatiently for five o'clock so she could switch the channel to the news. She liked this all women news show and watched it greedily until six o'clock when the male newscasters came on and rehashed the same stories with a delivery that said, *"This is the real news!"* It was time to take a bath and get ready for her date with Jared. She giggled as she turned the switch to off, collapsing the man to a thin white line.

As in the past two days, Jared was prompt, and she was waiting, dressed in a burnt orange silk suit. Jared smiled and complimented her warmly. She basked in his intimate look, convinced that tonight Jared would kiss her or make his intentions known. That's what she wanted, would like to happen, but she knew it wouldn't come to pass. Jared was acting just as polite and formal as he had acted on the other date. A small wave of panic washed over her as she saw him glance at the two cardboard cartons that were standing by the door, sealed with masking tape. She was thankful when he made no comment.

Jared brought her a glass of orange juice during the intermission of the play. She sipped at the tangy drink, wishing the night would never end. She loved it when Jared stood over her like this, staring down into her eyes. Her heart fluttered and then stilled. Nothing was going to happen, so it was unwise to even pretend it was. This was here and now and people like Jared Parsons didn't carry off people like Cathy Bissette. For a while he was enjoying her company or pretending to; it was good enough for now. "I'm leaving in the morning," he said quietly. Cathy's eyes widened at his words. She should say something. The words wouldn't come. Where was he going? Why was he going? She swallowed hard past the lump in her throat. Suddenly, the tart juice was sour, bitter to her tongue. With a trembling hand, she held out the glass to Jared. His expression was unreadable and Cathy suddenly felt terrified. After tonight she would never see him again. The lump in her throat was getting larger. How in the name of heaven was she going to get through the second half of the play? All she wanted to do was take off her shoes and run, run far and fast, and never look back.

"Ready?" Jared asked. Cathy nodded as Jared held her arm. It seemed to her that he was holding her much too tight then she realized she was quaking like an Aspen leaf and he was merely steadying her.

Thankful for the darkness of the theater, Cathy felt her body go limp with relief that now she could sit quietly and think. The figures on the stage held no magic for her, and she was barely aware of them or the presence of the audience around her. Jared was leaving.

He had to shake her arm twice before she was aware that the play was coming to an end. "Did you enjoy it?" Jared asked softly.

"Very much," Cathy lied. She hoped no one ever asked her how the play ended.

Somehow, on the ride back to her apartment, Cathy managed to make small conversation. They discussed the smog in New York and compared the teeming metropolis to Swan Quarter. Jared again complimented her on her suit by saying it was rare to see that particular shade and was it a favorite of blondes. Cathy nodded. She hated stupid, inane conversation. Why couldn't he say something interesting like: I love you. Come away with me; be mine. Oh, no, he had to talk about smog and suits the color of ripe persimmons. Men!

Jared paid the driver and tipped him generously. Cathy could tell the tip had been generous by the smile on the driver's face. And, he hadn't told him to wait. What did that mean?

"Do you mind if I come in for a few moments?" Jared asked, fitting the key in the lock.

"Please, I'd like that, but the only thing I can offer you is a glass of white wine or a cup of Chinese tea."

"Wine will be fine."

Cathy opened the kitchen cabinet for the glasses and winced. Two glasses, two Flintstone jelly glasses. Cathy poured the wine and carried both glasses into the living room. Jared accepted this, openly admiring Fred Flintstone who seemed to be dancing around the glass in purple garb. "Very original, Cathy," Jared said, pointing to the cartoon character on the glass.

Cathy's nerves were already on edge. She replied curtly, "All the other things are packed away."

"Packed away! Are you going somewhere?" Jared asked, his eyes going to the packed cartons by the door.

"I'm going back to Swan Quarter. I resigned the other day."

"Why didn't you tell me?" Jared asked quietly.

"I didn't think you would be interested in what I did. I'm sure it can't matter to you what I do or where I go." Please, she cried silently, say it matters.

"Is the big city too much for you to handle?"

"No. Not the city, the people. If you don't mind, I would rather not discuss it."

Jared drew her to him and cupped her chin in his hand. "Then we won't discuss it, it's as simple as that." He took possession of her mouth, his hands wound through her hair. His breath, feathered against her cheek, was wine-scented. She slid her hands inside his jacket, feeling the hard muscles of his chest and back, bringing him closer.

His lips traced the delicate line of her jaw and followed it to the softness behind her ear. She was losing herself in him, just like the night when they had been parked along the road in Swan Quarter. She heard the sudden intake of his breath and heard him murmur her name. The heavens descended around them; they were lost in the world of one another as his lips once again claimed hers.

She felt herself go weak as though she were dissolving into him.

He drew away from her and looked deeply into her eyes. His voice, when he spoke, was heavy with emotion and betrayed a passion that vibrated through her. There was open yearning in his voice and his eyes had become a flinty gray, burning deep into her being. "Heaven help me, Cathy, but I want you. And someday I mean to have you, but not like this."

Without further explanation, he rose and stalked to the door, opening it and shutting it behind him.

Chapter Eleven

Cathy's emergence back into Swan Quarter's busy life left much to be desired. She worked the trawler with Lucas until she was bone weary and exhausted. It was the only way she could sleep. Bizzy had taken to never letting her out of his sight. Where she went, Bizzy was right behind. He had even taken to sleeping at her bedside. He whined when she tossed and turned, sometimes stretching his long body to lick at her face.

All her dreams were of Jared, all her torments had him at their center. The last she had seen of him was his tall, straight back just before he had closed the door to her apartment behind him.

Why? Why had he left her that way? He had told her he wanted her and even now, after all this time, she still believed him. Still, a small voice tormented, wanting isn't loving.

The empty ache grew inside her. It was a familiar feeling now, almost like an old friend. Nothing had changed; she loved Jared Parsons.

There were so many unanswered questions, and she would probably never know the answers. But Jared was a man to be trusted, she knew this as well as she knew her own name. Nothing could ever take the memory of him away from her, and each time she felt her heart skip a beat when she thought of him, it somehow brought him closer. And if this longing and hunger was the price she must pay to keep him alive in her heart, pay it she would.

The days crawled into weeks and the weeks into months until it was nearing the Christmas season. Teak Helm's book was due. Was it out, was it in the local book store? Cathy pulled on her coat and headed for the pick-up truck, Bizzy at her side, barking his head off. "You can come, so stop it, you're giving me a headache," Cathy complained.

Cathy parked the truck and literally raced to the Book Nook, and there it was on display in the window. The *Sea Gypsy III*. Cathy frowned. That was the name of Jared Parson's boat. Well, she wasn't going to buy Helm's book. No way. She stared at it a minute longer with hungry eyes. It took every ounce of strength she possessed to walk away from the book store. Bismarc nudged her leg, hurrying her along. "Now, what is bothering you? Oh, I see, it's snowing. Okay, come on, we'll go home and hope it covers the ground and then we'll play."

The girl and the dog sat by the bow window far into the night, watching the miracle of fat flakes fall to the ground. "First thing in the morning we'll take a walk. Come on, Bizzy, time for bed."

It was a winter wonderland, the world, her part of the world anyway, was covered with a sparkling white blanket that dazzled her eyes. Quickly, she pulled on her boots and a heavy sheepskin jacket and opened the door for the setter, who leaped through it as though there was a bag of double Oreo cookies at the end of the walkway.

They ran, the girl and the dog, laughing and whooping in merriment. Bizzy tugged at her slacks, pulling her over into a heap. Cathy made one snowball after the other, tossing them to Bismarc who thought he was supposed to fetch. The moment he got the round ball in his mouth the snow fell apart and Cathy would throw another to the dog's delight.

"When are you going to make a snowman?" a quiet voice asked.

Startled, Cathy rolled over and then sat up. "Jared!" she cried in surprise. "What are you doing here? How did you get here? Are you staying?" Seeing him again this suddenly, without warning, sent a shock wave through her body. "Why are you looking at me like that? I'm a mess," she babbled as she brushed the snow from her clothes and then straightened her scarlet knitted cap. "Would you like to come back to the house for a cup of coffee?"

"Stop talking, Cathy," Jared said in a commanding voice. "Here, I brought you a present," he said, handing her a gift-wrapped package. "I want you to open it. Now!"

Puzzled, Cathy untied the gay ribbon and removed the gift wrapping. *"Sea Gypsy III!"* She felt all the color drain from her face as she stared at the title. Her lips trembled. "How could you be so cruel? How could you?" she cried heartbrokenly. She thrust the book at Jared and ran as if the hounds of hell were on her heels. Once she slipped and fell. Quickly, she righted herself but not before she saw Bismarc go after Jared, his teeth bared, snarls ripping from his throat. Jared was standing still, a helpless look on his face. "Let him go, Bizzy, he's not worth your time. Come on, boy." The setter let loose with a deep snarl and then ran after Cathy.

"Good boy, you gave him a good scare. I forgive all those other times," she cried, wrapping her arms around the wet setter. "I hate him, hate him, hate him!" she shrilled.

"No, you don't," Jared said, drawing her to her feet and holding her in his arms.

"Look at me. I love you. I've loved you from the minute I saw you sitting on your dock with your legs tucked under you. I even love that ridiculous dog of yours. I want you to marry me."

"Let me go! Your days of torturing me are over. I could forgive you almost anything but not that..." she said, pointing to the book Jared was holding.

"Open the book, Cathy, and read the dedication. I think that says it all. I'm Teak Helm. Now, do you understand?"

If Jared hadn't been holding Cathy, she would have slipped to the ground. Her vision was blurred, making it impossible to read the words. Jared read them for her: "For Cathy—this book needed her and I need her."

"But... you acted like, that time in the truck, Chunky, Erica. No, I don't believe you. Pneumonia. It's impossible," Cathy said in a dazed voice.

Jared's voice was tender and patient. "Cathy, I want you to look at me and believe everything I say to you. That time in the truck, I couldn't. You were too special. I didn't know just how special until that moment. I couldn't take advantage of you. If I had, you would have come to hate me. And as for that time when you saved Chunky, I had to be harsh with you. I had to make you angry so you would have the will to make it back to shore. There was no way I could have saved you both. Erica was never anything to me except a substitute secretary. Her sister is my regular secretary, but she had an appendectomy and Erica filled in for her till she came back to work."

"But what about this novel and Lefty..."

"I did not plagiarize Lefty Rudder. Lefty Rudder was my father. I was part of that sea adventure. In my father's book, if you remember, there was mention of a boy. I was that boy. The experience, the creative idea that you thought I stole from Lefty Rudder's book was my experience, the way I remembered it. Is there anything else?"

"You lied and said you were in the hospital," Cathy said, praying he had an answer.

"I was. I very foolishly discharged myself thinking I knew more than the doctors. I was wrong and I suffered for it. Is that it?" he grinned.

"You said I looked like I was sixteen."

"Darling girl, no sixteen-year-old ever looked like you. I knew you weren't sixteen. I swear it," he said, his eyes twinkling.

"Where have you been all this time? What took you so long to come for me?" her voice was choked with self-doubt.

Jared laughed. "It's all your fault. How could I turn in a manuscript that had the same difficulties as the last one. It had to be completely re-written. Walter Denuvue says you're back on as my editor. I told him you'd be working at home, from now on."

"Did my father know?"

"From the day he first came on my boat. He saw a sailing cup with Dad's name on it. He recognized it. I knew all about your father. Just the way your father told you stories of my father, mine told me stories of yours. They must have been some pair. Just like we're going to be. You will marry me, won't you?'' Jared asked anxiously.

Cathy moved closer into his embrace and brought her face up to his. ''Was there ever any doubt?'' Bismarc took that moment to race across the snow and sink his teeth into Jared's boot. ''Not now, Bizzy.'' The dog whined and then laid down as Jared bent his head to kiss Cathy.

* * * * *